SPECIAL MESSAGE TO READERS

This book is published under the auspices of

THE ULVERSCROFT FOUNDATION

(registered charity No. 264873 UK)

Established in 1972 to provide funds for research, diagnosis and treatment of eye diseases. Examples of contributions made are: —

A new Children's Assessment Unit at Moorfield's Hospital, London.

•

Twin operating theatres at the Western Ophthalmic Hospital, London.

•

A Chair of Ophthalmology at the University of Leicester.

•

The establishment of a Royal Australian College of Ophthalmologists "Fellowship".

You can help further the work of the Foundation by making a donation or leaving a legacy. Every contribution, no matter how small, is received with gratitude. Please write for details to:

THE ULVERSCROFT FOUNDATION,
The Green, Bradgate Road, Anstey,
Leicester LE7 7FU, England.
Telephone: (0116) 236 4325

In Australia write to:
THE ULVERSCROFT FOUNDATION,
c/o The Royal Australian College of Ophthalmologists,
27, Commonwealth Street, Sydney,
N.S.W. 2010.

Love is
a time of enchantment:
in it all days are fair and all fields
green. Youth is blest by it,
old age made benign:
the eyes of love see
roses blooming in December,
and sunshine through rain. Verily
is the time of true-love
a time of enchantment — and
Oh! how eager is woman
to be bewitched!

HINDSIGHT

This is the story of two young people who fell in love in the Second World War, parted and then met up again half a century later. As they tell each other what has happened to them in the intervening years, their respective life stories are vividly depicted in which sadness, regret and an insolvable mystery mingle with the constant realisation of 'what-might-have-been'. Both become astonished and grateful for the chance to make up for past mistakes and to start again — with hindsight.

Books by Pamela Street
in the Ulverscroft Large Print Series:

PERSONAL RELATIONS
THE BENEFICIARIES
THE TIMELESS MOMENT
PORTRAIT OF ROSE
LATE HARVEST

PAMELA STREET

HINDSIGHT

Complete and Unabridged

ULVERSCROFT
Leicester

First published in Great Britain in 1993 by
Robert Hale Limited
London

First Large Print Edition
published January 1995
by arrangement with
Robert Hale Limited
London

British Library CIP Data

Street, Pamela
Hindsight.—Large print ed.—
Ulverscroft large print series: romance
I. Title
823.914 [F]

ISBN 0–7089–3228–2

Published by
F. A. Thorpe (Publishing) Ltd.
Anstey, Leicestershire

Set by Words & Graphics Ltd.
Anstey, Leicestershire
Printed and bound in Great Britain by
T. J. Press (Padstow) Ltd., Padstow, Cornwall

This book is printed on acid-free paper

1

REX HARMAN fastened his seat belt and peered out of the window as the Boeing 747 lost height and touched down at Heathrow. He looked at his watch. One thirty p.m. Almost dead on time. Certainly a less hazardous and more predictable journey, he thought, than the one which had brought him to the Old Country in 1942. Then, as a GI, aged twenty-five, he had come down the gangplank of an American troopship docking at Belfast, grateful to be alive after an Atlantic crossing beset by storms and U-boats, wondering whether he would ever see his home ground again.

Rex collected up his hand baggage and waited, patiently, in the queue vacating the aircraft, courteously thanked the stewardess at the exit and started down the steps on to the runway, hoping that the hired car he had booked through a travel agency would be there to meet him.

It was. After he had picked up his other luggage and cleared customs, he was relieved to spot a man holding a placard saying 'Mr Rex Harman'. Some things worked, he told himself, as he settled into the back of a large Mercedes and gave himself up to watching the England of the 1990s flash by on either side of him in the pale sunlight of an October afternoon.

The man at the wheel waited, silently, for his passenger to make the first overture. Some liked to talk. Some didn't. Sam Barker had gauged, correctly, that Mr Harman would probably be in the former category and was not surprised when he heard Rex say, "I guess I'll be in for quite a few surprises since I was last here." After Sam had ascertained exactly when that was and the two of them had discovered that at the time one had been a small child evacuated from the bombed-out East End of London to a remote village in Wales and the other an American serviceman who had come over to Europe to 'hit Hitler for six', they kept up a lively conversation until their arrival at the Hilton.

Being a Sunday, and finding no Anna Linsdale in the telephone directory, Rex knew there was nothing else he could do about the object of his mission until the following day. After checking in to the hotel and being shown his room, he could think of nothing better to do than take himself off for a walk. He had been in London intermittently during the war, but he soon realised that the Park Lane which confronted him, with its heavy traffic and dual carriageway, was nothing like the one he had known in the 1940s. Yet, after he had negotiated one of the underpasses leading into Hyde Park, he felt on more familiar ground. Somehow there was the same feel about the place. There might not be many people wearing uniform nor any evidence of air-raid shelters and the railings had all been put back, but it was still the green oasis he remembered, the *rus in urbe* in a land for which he was pleased to have fought.

Now, half a century later, he sat down on one of the seats and took out a book, a paperback he had kept in his pocket ever since he had come upon it quite by chance one day, while waiting at O'Hare airport. It was called *Aftermath* by Anna Linsdale. There was no photograph on the cover, as there might have been if it was a hardback; but there was a brief biographical sketch which assured him it was the Anna he knew, that this was her first novel, such information ending, somewhat cryptically, with the words: *The author lives in London*.

Well, he was in London now, wasn't he? He had travelled half way across the world to see Anna Linsdale again. He could have contacted her through her publishers, he supposed, written Anna a letter, as he had done many a time in 1943 and again in 1944, just before D-Day. But his letters were never answered. He decided he wasn't going to go through any of that again. He would simply arrive on her doorstep. He realised that she could be married, divorced, widowed, faded, fat or even ill. But he had to see her. He wanted to put the record straight. Get to the bottom of her sudden strange rejection of him after they had once been so close. He had the money now, as well as the freedom, to act on a whim. Besides, he hadn't had a proper holiday since his wife, Rosalind, had died — nor for a long time before that.

Poor Ros. Once, at the beginning of her illness, she had come across a photograph of Anna at the back of a drawer in his desk. He had cursed himself for leaving it there, as she wormed the story out of him. As the years passed and she became more and more handicapped, she had seemed to become obsessed by what she called, 'the love of your life'. In a way, he supposed Ros was right, although he had told her over and over again that he and Anna had never had an affair, and that he had neither seen nor heard from her after they parted in 1943.

Sometimes, frightened of losing him, when he was a little late returning from the tall Chicago skyscraper where he managed the large estate of the McCutcheon family, she would start accusing him of having other affairs. "But Honey," he would begin, and then she would round on him, "I suppose you called your English inamorata 'Honey'?"

"No," he would answer, truthfully. "I never called her 'Honey'." He did not add that sometimes he had murmured a few more intimate terms of endearment. He had wanted Anna Linsdale as he had never wanted any other woman, before or since. He had been totally in love with her and he had had a fairly good idea that she felt the same way about him, even though she had hinted at another relationship with an English army officer, a prisoner of war in Germany.

He had always remembered how, one summer evening, when he had been on a long and gruelling exercise on Dartmoor, he had come back to the small Dorset town where he was stationed and, as telephone calls were never allowed, he had cycled straight to the Emergency Hospital where Anna was working as a VAD. Outside in the courtyard he had waylaid another nurse and asked her if she could tell him where Anna was or when she might be off duty. The girl had stared at him. "Anna Linsdale's left," she said. "*Left*?" he repeated, frowning, and his informant had simply replied, "Yes. Look, I must dash. The sisters here are battle-axes. There's all hell to pay if you're late coming on nights." Rex had stood there in the fading light, a tall thin figure, a man with an expression of stunned bewilderment on his handsome face.

Suddenly, galvanised into action, he had leapt on his bicycle and ridden the ten miles to Anna's home, an old grey stone rectory in the village of Withyford. He had never cared very much for visiting Anna's parents, although he had soon become aware that convention made it necessary. English girls were somewhat behind the times compared to their American counterparts when it came to dating. Anna would never be allowed to go out with a young man whom the Reverend and Mrs Linsdale had not vetted. Of the two of them, Rex had always far preferred Anna's father, a gentle saintly-looking man who seemed genuinely interested in his guest and in hearing what life was like, as he referred to it, 'over the water'.

Mrs Linsdale was different altogether. Rex sensed that, despite an effort to please, she distrusted him. She would lay on a good meal, so far as rationing permitted, but he sometimes caught her looking at him speculatively, and he felt uneasy when left alone in her presence. There was no doubt who wore the trousers in the household. Often, Rex wondered what strange alchemy had brought this grey-haired taciturn woman and her frail kindly husband together. Even more often, he wondered how they had ever managed to produce such an astonishingly lovely and lively daughter. Tonight, as he propped his bicycle against the rectory gatepost, he hoped it would not be Janet Linsdale who answered the door.

Sadly, his hopes were dashed. "Anna?" he blurted out, without preamble, as he stood before her, feeling a little as if he were being hauled up before his commanding officer.

"Anna is not here, Captain Harman." Janet had never called him by his Christian name.

"Not here? Where . . . is she ill?"

"No. She decided, rather than continuing to work as a VAD, she would be more useful taking a full nurses' training. She has been transferred to a teaching hospital."

"But . . . I mean . . . When? It must have been a very sudden decision."

"Yes. But when Anna makes up her mind, she acts quickly. There was no difficulty at the Emergency Hospital. They happen to be slack there at the moment. The authorities are only too pleased when a girl decides to take nursing seriously. Make it her career. It will certainly stand her in good stead after the war."

After the war. God knew when that would be. Why, he had hoped by then that he and Anna might . . . well, he hadn't dared to think about it too much, knowing he had so little to offer her, that he had never, like some of his contemporaries, settled into a steady job. Although the last time they had been together, he had been about to tell her what was in his mind. Miserably, he now remained standing at the front door of the rectory. He noticed that Janet Linsdale made no attempt to ask him in.

"May I have Anna's address, please?" he said, at length.

Then the woman before him came out with her extraordinary answer. "There are various teaching hospitals in this country, Captain Harman. You must make your own enquiries. But I think I must warn you that my daughter specifically asked me not to give you her address."

2

LADY MALLINDER, standing in the hallway of her small Kensington flat, called to her granddaughter, "Hurry up, Chloe. We'll be late back at Atherstone Lodge if we don't get a move on."

"Coming, Grandma." Chloe Mallinder came flying along the passage from her bedroom, a thin, pretty, scatterbrained ten-year-old. "But I'm still looking for my clarinet. Oh, where *is* it, Gran?"

"Here." Anna Mallinder picked up a case by the front door and handed it to her. Then, with one of those sudden disarming displays of affection and gratitude, Chloe flung her arms round her grandmother, saying, "Oh, *thank* you. I don't know what I'd do without you, Gran."

Anna Mallinder smiled. "I expect you'd learn much faster how to look after yourself and your belongings, my dear. Now, come *on*."

They went down in the lift and out into the dark October night, where Anna's car was parked a little way away. Depositing all Chloe's paraphernalia in the boot, they got inside, adjusted their seat belts and set off.

Slowly and carefully, Anna edged out of Stanhope Gardens into the Cromwell Road. She never enjoyed these Sunday night journeys, especially at this time of the year. She was sixty-nine and, though still a beautiful, even elegant woman, the life she had led had taken its toll. There were deep lines under the large brown eyes, a tenseness about the tall lean figure. Surprisingly, however, although her dark hair was not as thick and luxurious as once it had been, there was only a hint of grey at the temples.

It was less than twenty miles to Chloe's weekly boarding-school in Surrey and sometimes Anna wondered whether she had been right to opt for Atherstone Lodge, whether it might not have been better to have kept Chloe at day-school in London for a few more years and then, perhaps, sent her right away to boarding-school. But the beauty of Atherstone was that the girl could stay there until the age of eighteen, Anna would still see her every weekend and she also happened to know the headmistress.

In the end, the decision was more or less taken for her by her GP, Dr Fenton. "Look," he had said, "your flat is not exactly large, Anna. Much as I know that you love Chloe and she loves you, I think it would be better if, during the week, she lived with children of her own age. You've done a splendid job since . . ." he hesitated, "well, since you took on, but it wouldn't do for the generations to be quite so much on top of one another. Chloe is rather a headstrong child. She needs, or will need, a firm hand, if you don't mind my saying so. You'd maintain a far better relationship if you simply enjoyed each other's company at weekends. Besides, you've got your own work to think about. After the success of *Aftermath*, you're surely going to keep at it."

So far, Anna had to admit that Dr Fenton had been right. Chloe did seem happy in spite of all the tragedy in her young life. Maybe the fact that she *had* been so young meant that she had managed to accept and adapt to all that had happened, had taken it for granted that her grandmother would look after her. Tonight, she prattled on cheerfully about this and that: her music, her art and the *surprise* she would have for Anna at Christmas. "You'll never guess, Gran," she kept saying, "never in a million years." And Anna had replied, "Chloe, please, don't be so tantalising. I can't wait."

On her return journey that night Anna wondered just what Chloe had in store for her. Something she had made, presumably. Soon, she herself must think about Christmas and Christmas presents: finding a better clarinet which she knew Chloe wanted, arranging dental and eye appointments — Chloe was slightly short-sighted like Anna — tickets for *The Wind in The Willows*, a party of some sort. The holidays always seemed to go by in a flash. Anna never attempted to write during them. Sometimes she wondered how she had ever managed to complete *Aftermath* once Chloe had come to live with her. But in many ways it had been therapeutic. She had never expected it to be published. But it gave her something to do after she had taken the child to day-school each morning. She would shut herself up in her bedroom and work, relying on Maria, her daily Portuguese cleaner, to see to the rest of the chores.

Since the book's publication, Anna was not at all sure she had the ability to write another one, however much encouragement she kept receiving. Looking back, she felt that there had been a curious inevitability about having written *Aftermath*, although the success, coming to her so late in life, seemed not only overwhelming but somehow scary.

Tonight, after she got home, Anna poured herself a whisky and soda — a treat she felt she could now safely indulge in — and sat looking over the London skyline. Although the drink revived her a little, she felt tired, old. She seemed to have lived a long time, to have come a long way since the shy immature girl who had once, so it would appear from photographs, looked a little like her granddaughter. What would life hold for Chloe? Probably she would never know. When the child had said earlier that evening, "I don't know what I'd do without you, Gran," she could not possibly have guessed how close she had got to the fear which was constantly in Anna's mind. What *would* Chloe do? True, she had made the child's godfather, Geoffrey Sheldon, a guardian and had left her entire estate — apart from a few small bequests — in trust for her. But please God she would live long enough to see Chloe through her schooldays and able to look after herself.

But could she at, say, eighteen? Dr Fenton had already hinted at a certain waywardness, an unpredictability. Anna knew, of course, that Chloe was growing up in a world very different from that of her own childhood. Chloe was already far more mature than she had been at that age. She thought of her own *naïveté*, her gaucheness, her ignorance of sex, of men in general and, later on, her inability to handle them. Despite her looks, there had really only been two of them in her life: her husband whom she had married at the end of the war and who, after five years in captivity, had been more or less a stranger; and the young American Rex Harman, to whom she had completely lost her heart and maybe, just as easily, could have lost her virginity. She could see him now with startling clarity the last time they had been together picnicking by the woods on the downs above Withyford. She knew her mother had not approved, remembered how grudging she had been when Anna had asked for some spam for their sandwiches, how Janet Linsdale had admonished her to be home by nine.

It had been getting on for that time when, the picnic finished, Anna had lain back on the short springy turf. The sun had been going down, there was the scent of wild thyme in the air and she recalled a thrill such as she had never known before or since when Rex, too, had lain down and started kissing her. But for Lizzie Maidment, one of her father's middle-aged parishioners, who had suddenly appeared from the woods with her small dog, would Rex have . . . would she have let him? It had been something on which she had pondered ever afterwards. But one thing was quite certain. Lizzie Maidment had put an end to any lovemaking.

When, afterwards, Anna had tried to look at the situation more objectively, she managed to persuade herself that maybe Lizzie Maidment's intervention had been providential. The woman had probably saved her from a fate worse than death. She might have become pregnant, just like all those girls on the new council estate on the outskirts of Withyford. It seemed that unmarried mothers with babies in prams were becoming the norm in the village. Her mother had shown an unnaturally prurient interest in them, Anna thought, although never, so far as she could recall, her father. He had simply gone about his parochial duties, busier than ever, continually counselling the poor angry mothers of the 'fallen' — as Janet Linsdale referred to them — who appeared with singular regularity at the side door of the rectory, railing against Hitler, the Americans and rationing, all in one breath.

On her days off from the hospital Anna had been aware of this state of affairs, but remote from it. Such troubles as befell the Mavis Hapgoods, the Della Shergolds or the Audrey Musselwhites were, in the very nature of things, something which happened to those who came from another stratum of society. It was not that Anna was a snob or considered herself above them, simply that she had been brought up differently. She was the rector's daughter, immune, as she thought, from the temptations to which the girls in the Withyford council houses — or, for that matter, the old cottages — were exposed. For all her intelligence, she had never thought to question the status quo, to have imagined that Mavis, Della, Audrey and she herself were all sisters under the skin.

After the Rex episode she learned, perhaps, one of the most important lessons in her whole life. She was a woman with ordinary feelings, ordinary desires. She could well have become 'up the spout', a term she had heard, dismissed as vulgar and nothing to do with her. Now, she thought of it with increasing horror. After all, it was she, wasn't it, who had actually initiated the picnic, had wanted, without knowing exactly why, to be somewhere quite alone with Rex Harman. The possibility of pregnancy, the awakening of a passion she had hitherto not known she possessed, the disgrace she might have brought on her parents, haunted her and propelled her into a course of action which, though certainly encouraged and approved by Janet Linsdale and possibly commendable for showing a certain strength of character, was, she felt in retrospect, far less commendable for the ruthless, almost insensitive, way it was carried out.

3

REX HARMAN walked over to the desk in the entrance hall of Anna's publishers and asked for her address. Having failed to get anywhere with them on the telephone, he had decided on the direct approach. The girl before him had not been with the firm long, but she knew enough to reply, "I'm sorry, sir, but we do not disclose our authors' addresses."

Rex frowned. Now that he had arrived in person he had not expected this setback. "Can I see whoever's in charge here?" he persisted. "Your chairman, perhaps?"

This time it was Hilary Smith who frowned. "I'm sorry, sir," she said again, "but he's not here today. Perhaps you would like to speak to his secretary, Miss Morland."

"Certainly," Rex replied. "Which floor?"

"If you would just wait over there, sir, I will try to contact her office."

Hilary Smith then proceeded to press various switches and, after a short conversation, informed Rex that Miss Morland would be down to see him. He wondered why he couldn't go up and see her. They were making him feel as if he were attempting to storm Fort Knox or, at least, infiltrate some security building. Surely there was nothing wrong with his perfectly innocent request.

Presently, some swing doors opened and an attractive well-groomed young woman came through them, smiling pleasantly. Rex decided that perhaps it was time to be a little less aggressive. He smiled back. "Rex Harman, ma'am," he said, rising and holding out his hand which was courteously taken, "enquiring after the whereabouts of one of your authors."

"So I understand, Mr Harman. But I'm afraid it isn't possible to let you have Miss Linsdale's address."

Rex's smile faded somewhat. "But I don't quite understand, Miss Morland."

"We have a duty to protect our authors," she continued. "It is the firm's policy. I think you would find that this pertains in any publishing house. If you would just write to Miss Linsdale at this address, we will certainly see that your letter is forwarded to her."

Rex Harman suddenly drew himself up to his full height, aware that he stooped a little these days. He still spoke pleasantly but with deliberation. "Ma'am, I dare say I could write. I dare say I could have done so back in the States. But I decided that I wanted to pay a surprise visit on Miss Linsdale. I have travelled half way across the world in order to do this. You can call me eccentric if you like, but I assure you I am not a nutcase or anyone from whom you evidently feel Miss Linsdale needs protection. I knew her getting on for half a century ago. In the Second World War. For reasons it would take too long to go into here, I couldn't come back to the Old Country before. But now I have." He pulled *Aftermath* out of his pocket. "I don't know if you've read this book, but if you have you might just understand why I'm doing what I'm doing."

Fiona Morland became disconcerted. She hadn't actually read *Aftermath*, although her boss had recommended it as an unusual love story. Certainly, Mr Harman didn't look like a lunatic. A romantic, perhaps. She pictured him in the last war, so far as her imagination allowed. It was so long before her time. Something her grandparents had talked about. Mr Harman must have been smashing in uniform. He was still very handsome. Quite a guy, in fact, with his height, charm and Gregory Peck looks. She thought of Anna Mallinder and how nice it would be for her to see him again, but she couldn't . . . she didn't dare go against company policy. Why, Mr Pemberton would fire her. of course, she could ask Dave Mason. She knew Dave rather fancied her.

"If you'd care to wait a little longer, Mr Harman," she said, "I will see if there is anyone else who could help you."

Fiona Morland walked back through the swing doors. A neat figure, Rex thought, watching her. He had always had an eye for a pretty woman. She was only doing her duty, he supposed.

After a few minutes she returned and asked if he would accompany her in the lift to the office of one of their senior editors. "Mr Mason," she explained, confidentially, "*edits* Miss Linsdale."

"Edits?" Rex enquired, raising an eyebrow, aware that Miss Morland seemed to be wearing some rather pleasing scent.

"Yes. Well, I mean . . . all our authors have editors who . . ."

"Edit," Rex broke in.

Fiona Morland could not help laughing then. The lift stopped. She ushered him into Dave Mason's office, where a tall bespectacled youth rose to greet him, who Rex judged to be still in his twenties.

When they were both seated, Anna's editor said, "I understand you want Miss Linsdale's address, sir?"

"I sure do."

"It is not usual, Mr Harman. In fact, we never divulge personal information of this kind."

"But you've said here," Rex answered, pulling *Aftermath* out of his pocket once more and turning to the back cover, *"Anna Linsdale was brought up in the West Country, the only daughter of a rector in a village near Dorchester. She nursed during the Second World War but did not take up writing until a few years ago. This, her first novel, has had an outstanding success both in England and abroad. She now lives in London.* Why say that," Rex asked, a trifle belligerently, "if you're so keen to protect her whereabouts?"

"London is a large place, Mr Harman," replied Dave Mason, in an effort to be diplomatic. "Any letter you send here will be forwarded and then Miss Linsdale can decide for herself whether . . . "

Rex stared at the young man behind the desk, a mere stripling, he thought, who had known nothing, absolutely *nothing* about the Second World War. A child, in fact, born in the swinging sixties most likely, who now probably knew all about drugs and Aids and computers, the fall of the Berlin Wall and the end of communism. That was quite a chunk of history to assimilate, he supposed. Perhaps he should not feel quite so superior or censorious.

"Look, Mr Mason," he broke in, more kindly. "I appreciate your evident concern for Miss Linsdale's welfare. But I assure you I am no threat. It's just that I knew her a long, a very long time ago before you were born. I decided, after reading *Aftermath*, it would be good to see her again and, as I told Miss Morland, I have travelled some twelve thousand miles, I guess, to pay my respects in person. It may seem quixotic, but perhaps I'm of a generation which does quixotic things. I might add that, without wishing to presume, it has occurred to me that Miss Linsdale might not have written *Aftermath* if it hadn't been for me."

There was silence then between them, except for the sound of typing in the next room. Dave Mason wondered whether to put his visitor on to Anna's agent but suddenly decided to take a chance. Even though *Aftermath* had been set in another era, he had always felt that the novel had more than a ring of truth about it. He supposed that was why it had been such a success. It was intriguing to think he might be confronting one of the chief characters.

"She lives in Kensington, Mr Harman," he said. "Stanhope Gardens. Number 18. Top Flat."

Rex stood up. He leaned forward slightly, almost as if he were giving an old-fashioned bow. "Thank you," he said, "I am much obliged."

Dave Mason also rose. They faced each other, the older man with seventy-five years of experience behind him, the younger one yet to make his way, but full of the hope with which youth invariably seemed endowed. Rex remembered his own so well. Even in the war, going across the Channel on D-Day in one of those ghastly flat-bottomed boats on June 6th, 1944. One was scared stiff and yet, somehow death wasn't exactly on the agenda. One was too hyped up, the adrenalin flowing, so many things to see to. There was a job to do. He was a major then, in charge. But suddenly, inexplicably, just as he was wading ashore, a picture of Anna Linsdale as he had last seen her, flashed into his mind. He had come from the States to fight for England, for the liberation of Europe, but he had also known, in that minute, he was fighting for the safety of the girl he would never forget.

"Anna Linsdale," he heard Dave

Mason now saying, and Rex was so wrapped up in the past, that the young man's voice seemed to come from a long way off, along the airwaves from another age, another time, "writes under her maiden name, of course. I know little about her private life. Only that she is Lady Mallinder and a widow."

4

WHEN the bell in the street rang in Anna's flat on Monday morning, she let Maria answer it. She was not expecting any callers and was surprised when the girl knocked on her bedroom door and announced that there was a gentleman asking for Lady Mallinder.

Anna frowned. Her writing was not going well these days. She felt she would never be able to follow up the success of *Aftermath*. She found herself apt to pick on any excuse for not 'keeping at it', as Dr Fenton, Dave Mason and her agent, Tim Parker, kept advocating. Because of this she had managed to get an early appointment with her hairdresser that day, often finding that a wash and set was conducive to the thought processes. Blood to the head, she would say to herself, wryly, yet it sometimes worked. Now, back at her typewriter again — she had never ceased to be thankful she had learned to type on coming to London — she did not want to be disturbed.

"Did he give his name, Maria?"

"No. He just said he wanted Lady Mallinder."

Still frowning, Anna went into the hallway and picked up the intercom. The beauty about this arrangement was that she was never obliged to let anyone in. One could press the buzzer which automatically opened the street door, or not. Certainly, she would never admit a total stranger into the building.

"Yes?" She was aware of sounding a little short.

There was a barely perceptible pause and then an American voice said, "Anna. This is Rex."

She did not say anything. She simply pressed the buzzer, as if she might have been expecting him. Then she opened her front door and waited while the old-fashioned lift bore him upwards, and the ridiculous thing about those few moments, she remembered afterwards, was that all she could think of was how glad she felt that she had just had her hair done.

Suddenly, the lift came to a halt. The doors opened and he stepped out on to the landing. The gap of fifty years seemed to close up, like a concertina, blotting out any memory of time in between. He gave her a mock salute. "May I come in?"

"Of course."

She led him into the sitting-room, thankful that Maria had just finished her daily chores and was about to go home.

For several minutes they sat in silence until it dawned on Anna that the least she could do would be to offer him a drink. "Later," was all he said. "Right now, I'd sooner . . . well . . . just look at you."

She found herself blushing and put up a hand to her face to hide the fact. "Fifty years is a long time, Rex."

"Only yesterday," he answered. "Only yesterday. You're even more beautiful than I remember."

She wondered how to reply. She had never been good at receiving compliments. Should she tell him that he himself was amazingly well-preserved, even more handsome than she, too, remembered?

No, it wasn't in her nature. Besides, it would be too much like embarking on some mutual admiration caper and she knew he wouldn't want that.

Suddenly, he said, "Why exactly *did* you stand me up, Anna?"

She looked away. "Didn't you guess?"

"No. That is, not until I read *Aftermath*. I suppose it gave me some idea, but it wasn't like you to be so . . . well, unpredictable. I wondered whether your mother . . . " He broke off, a little embarrassed, before continuing, "Incidentally, I loved the book, Anna."

"Thank you, Rex." Then, conscious that she still had not answered his question, she said, "It wasn't my mother's doing. She might not have wanted our relationship to continue. Indeed, she said so in no uncertain terms, but the decision to sever it completely and at once was entirely mine. I realise I acted monstrously and I often wondered if I could ever be forgiven, but . . . you see, I was afraid of you."

"Afraid?"

"Yes. Well, more afraid of myself,

perhaps. I suppose it sounds incomprehensible now. I mean, when one thinks of today's youth."

When he did not answer, she went on, quietly, "You see, I wanted you to make love to me."

"Was that so very terrible?"

"Fifty years ago and in the way I was brought up, yes."

Now it was his turn to look away. Presently, he said, "I'd decided, you know, during that picnic to ask you to marry me, even though I had nothing to offer you, materially, that is. I knew there would be opposition from your mother, but I felt it could be overcome. I believe your father would have given us his blessing. I felt that you were as in love with me as I was with you. Somehow, sex didn't seem all that wrong in the circumstances. Whether, that evening, we would have . . . I don't know. But I do know that I never really forgave that old harridan with her dog for appearing when she did."

Anna smiled. "Afterwards, I kept trying to tell myself that she probably saved me from . . ."

He broke in. "Didn't you think I'd stand by you, Anna?"

She flushed again. Defensively she replied, "Rex, I knew so little about you. You never said much about yourself. For all I knew, you might have had . . ."

"A wife back home? Many of us did, I suppose. But no, I was fancy free. I didn't mean to fall for an English girl, certainly not ask one to marry me. But then, you, you were different from anyone else I'd ever met. Standing in front of you in the Paul Jones at that tea dance . . . well, it seemed fate that the music stopped just when it did. The band went on to play *Deep Purple*, remember?"

"Yes, I remember," she answered, barely audibly. Once or twice, when it was played on the radio and Chloe was with her, the child had remarked, "You do look sad, Gran, when that tune is played," and Anna had replied, "Do I?" and switched it off.

"How did you find me, Rex?" she continued.

"Through reading *Aftermath*."

"You mean you wrote to my publishers?"

"No. I just came on over. I went to see them first thing this morning. They didn't want to let me have your address, but in the end I got it out of them."

She looked at him, incredulously.

"I wasn't going to bother with letters," he went on. "After all, you weren't exactly good at answering mine after we last met, if I remember rightly."

For the third time the colour came to her cheeks. "But I mightn't have been here," she said. "Actually, I had to do quite a bit of travelling to promote the book when it first came out."

"Well, if you weren't at home, that would have been just too bad. But I reckoned I'd take a chance. Besides, I'd have waited. I needed a holiday. I wanted to see England again. Will you show it to me, Anna? Drive down to the West Country, maybe. Unless you have . . . other commitments, of course?"

"I do have one. My granddaughter. She comes here every weekend."

"Today is only Monday, Anna."

She became confused. It had been such an ordinary start to the week. She knew that her engagement diary, never very full, had little in it other than a lunch with a friend on Wednesday — easily postponable — and she had promised herself she would start some Christmas shopping before she fetched Chloe from Atherstone on Friday. She supposed she must lead what most people would consider an extremely dull life nowadays. She rarely went out in the evenings. They were mostly given over to looking, with dissatisfaction, at anything she might have written earlier on, listening to the news, reading or doing the crossword puzzle. Often, she was in bed by nine.

"Don't say no, Anna," she heard Rex continue. "I guess at our time of life we could simply be fellow travellers. You're a widow and I'm a widower. What was the title of the book one of your famous authors wrote? J. B. Priestley, I believe. Dead, I imagine, now. Ah yes, *The Good Companions*. We'd have three clear days, and two halves if we left this afternoon. I'd so much like to see Withyford again. I'll hire a car. I've got an international licence."

To her astonishment, she found herself saying, "There would be no need.

Wouldn't mine do? It's insured for any driver."

His face lit up. "If you'd trust me to be your chauffeur, Ma'am. I might be a bit out of touch with your left-hand side of the road, but I shouldn't go too fast. I imagine the hotels wouldn't be too booked up at this time of the year. We could get a couple of rooms. Is the Withyford Arms still functioning, do you know?"

Oddly enough, she had read somewhere recently that it had been restored and enlarged and could be recommended as an excellent place to stay for those wanting a comfortable quiet holiday in the West Country. She had thought to herself: why don't I go there one weekend. Take Chloe. See the rectory. And then she had thought: no, don't go back. What good would it do? The past is the past.

"We could go over the past," Rex said. "Fill in the gaps. You could tell me what happened to you after we last saw each other and, if you're interested, I could tell you what happened to me."

5

IT did not take her long to pack. By 4 p.m. that day they were having tea in Salisbury. In the fading light, Rex said, "Good heavens, what's all that scaffolding doing on top of the cathedral spire?" and Anna had explained about the enormous efforts being taken in connection with its much-needed restoration.

"I'm glad," he answered. "I remember passing through here on the way to the coast just before D-Day and thinking: that's something, please God, which must be preserved at all costs, something to fight for, amongst other things."

They had managed to book two separate rooms at the Withyford Arms and she had telephoned Atherstone Lodge to let the school know her whereabouts until Friday. It had always been like this ever since Chloe had come under her care. The child had priority. She must feel secure, know that Anna would be there, only a telephone call away.

She and Rex had not spoken a great deal on the journey, except to make the briefest references to their respective pasts. She sensed he wanted to concentrate on his driving and mutual silence seemed perfectly natural. There was no awkward constraint between them. Nor did they say very much after they set off again. By then, it was dark and she was content to sit beside him, while a curious peace came over her. But a few miles short of Withyford, he said, "I guess you'd better direct me now. Don't we turn off quite soon?"

"Yes. Just past the next roundabout. Although it all looks rather different to me."

"You've never been back?"

"No. Not after my father died and my mother left the district."

"Never wanted to?"

"Not really. At least, not until now."

He gave her a quick smile.

Once they had arrived in the village, checked in at the Withyford Arms, and arranged to meet later in the bar, she almost lost her way locating it. The place was like nothing she remembered, not that she had often been there. It would never have done for the rector's daughter to have been seen drinking in any bar, especially with an American GI. Oddly enough, the few times she had been inside the establishment were when her father had given her lunch there once or twice when her mother was away and then, in 1945, when the man she was about to marry put up there for a week. She recalled it being cold and uncomfortable — full of wartime restrictions and statutory five shilling meals because of rationing — very different from the present ambience on which some expert had evidently spent a lot of time, trouble and money. There was nothing to remind her of her youth. Even the sign outside proclaiming its name, lit up by coloured lights, only gave her a faint sense of having been there before.

Yet at dinner that night she experienced a less obvious but far more poignant link with the past. For a while, she was unable to understand why she kept puzzling over the identity of the girl who waited on them. After all, she knew no one in

Withyford now and had not done so for many years. But every time the girl came to their table Anna felt as if memory was holding out on her, refusing to yield a secret.

Then it dawned on her: those big blue eyes, that wide loose mouth. It was a face which could only belong to a Shergold. She must be related to the family, maybe a granddaughter of Della, whose mother had come to the rectory one night and started cursing about a GI, who had put Della 'in the family way'. Anna recalled that it had been that scene more than any other which had haunted her after her picnic with Rex. For the first time since they had left London she felt embarrassed and was aware that he had noticed. She realised that little escaped him. There was a sensitivity about him which she had failed to appreciate before.

"What's bothering you, Anna?"

"It's our waitress. I think I knew her family. Name of Shergold."

"Shall we ask her?"

She hesitated. "Not now. Maybe tomorrow. There was trouble," she went on quickly. "A child out of wedlock. It was happening all the time."

"Because of my fellow countrymen, I guess."

"Not always, by any means," she assured him. But Anna recalled that the whole village seemed to know who the father of Della's baby was, a large fat corporal with whom the girl had been walking out and, most likely, been caught in *flagrante* by Lizzie Maidment or other busybodies, whose hitherto dull narrow existences had been greatly enlivened by keeping a constant watch on the activities of the younger generation, rather as the older men in the Withyford Home Guard waited — and even hoped — for a chance of dealing with German enemies.

Rex was silent for a while and then he remarked, "It's strange when you come to think about it. I mean, today we have the pill, abortion and Aids, but in those days it was . . . "

"Illegitimacy," she continued for him, "or the fear of it. But we wouldn't even call it that now. A mother with a child but without a husband would simply be a one-parent family. The stigma has gone."

He stared at her, miserably. “Oh, Anna, I’m so very sorry. Even after reading *Aftermath*, I never quite realised . . . I should have been more straightforward . . . told you more about myself . . . ”

“There’s still time,” she replied, gently. “That’s what we’re here for, isn’t it? To catch up. Put the record straight. I’m looking forward to hearing all about Rex Harman both before and after I met him.”

“Of course. But won’t you begin? Let’s go into the lounge.”

After they had found a secluded corner, he went on, “That night after I last saw you running into the rectory. What exactly happened?”

She thought for a moment and then replied, flatly, “I went to bed. I remember my mother coming out into the hall and calling up something about my being late. I had to get back to the hospital the following evening ready to go on night duty. But before I left, Lizzie Maidment had done her damnedest. She came to the rectory next morning. I saw her out of my bedroom window. I was up there hoping to get a bit of sleep because I hadn’t had any during the night. I knew why she'd come. Then my mother came up and knocked on my door and said, 'I'd like an explanation, Anna, of your behaviour last evening.' I didn't answer. I mean, I knew I hadn't actually done anything wrong, although I felt awfully guilty for having led you on. Then my mother said that Miss Maidment had felt it her duty to let her know that her daughter had been caught in a most compromising position and that there was no doubt I was in grave danger. My mother started working herself up into almost a frenzy then. I'd never seen her so angry, but I honestly think it was the fact that Lizzie Maidment had told her about us that really upset her most. After she had finished saying that I was no better than I should be, she ended her tirade by saying I was never to see Captain Harman again."

"But I thought you said that it wasn't your mother who stopped you seeing me."

"No. It wasn't. Besides, I suppose with some young girls her attitude might have produced the opposite effect. But I'd already made up my own mind. I knew

I wouldn't be able to go on seeing you without . . . well, what I was afraid of . . . happening. I told my mother she needn't worry, that I was going to give in my notice at the hospital as soon as I got back and that I'd decided to ask to be transferred to a London teaching one, where I could take a full nurses' training. I shall never forget the look on her face. There was a kind of triumph in it or, possibly, self-satisfaction. It was almost as if she was pleased I was going through it. I never knew until a long time later just why."

"You know I tracked you down, that I called at the nurses' home? And you must have got my letters."

"Yes. Oh, Rex, looking back, I behaved so unkindly, so discourteously. But I kept telling myself it was the only way."

He put a hand over hers. "Don't castigate yourself, Anna. I was just as much to blame. Tell me, what was it like at St Thomas's?"

"Pretty good hell."

"Didn't you have any fun? Go out with someone else? Surely there must have been some recreation."

"Not really. At least, not for me. I sort of shut up shop, if you understand the expression. I felt terribly tired most of the time, only too grateful to get back to the nurses quarters at the end of the day and go to bed. Even on my days off."

"Sounds a very unnatural life for a young girl, especially one as pretty as you."

She smiled. "Thank you for the compliment. I suppose it was rather odd. But, apart from anything else, I began feeling not only guilty about you but also about the young man in the prison camp I once told you about. He kept writing and I felt obliged to write back. He said most of his companions had received what he called rejection slips from their girlfriends and he was so pleased he hadn't had one from me, that it was good to feel I was still waiting."

"And were you?"

"No. I was horrified. He had obviously taken our innocent relationship much more seriously than I had. You must think me awfully stupid, Rex, but I simply became confused. There was no one I felt I could talk to about it all.

Whenever I went home on leave my mother always asked if I'd heard from that 'poor nice prisoner-of-war friend'. She made me want to scream. I think my father understood a great deal more about the situation but, of course, he never said anything. My mother saw to that. I knew one reason why she was so keen on Dick Mallinder was because his father was a baronet and she knew that one day Dick would inherit the title."

"Oh, God," Rex said. "But surely that didn't cut any ice with you?"

"No. Of course it didn't. But, incredible as it may seem to you today, I felt I'd already behaved badly to one young man, you, and I didn't have the heart to behave badly to another, in a totally different way. The whole thing got me down so much that I ended up in another hospital — as a patient."

"Oh, God," Rex said again.

6

"I WANT to hear more," Rex said, "about this illness you had."

They were sitting on an old tree stump at the edge of the woods above Withyford, very near to the same spot where they had had their last ill-fated meeting. It was a cold clear October morning, the sky a pale icy blue; in the distance they could just see a patch of darker blue where it melted into the English Channel. At breakfast, they had only spoken of trivialities, knowing that mutual reminiscences would begin later on. Their waitress of the previous evening was nowhere to be seen.

"I'm sorry," Anna replied, firmly, "but it's your turn." Apart from anything else she had no wish to talk about her breakdown, although she realised she would have to do so sometime.

"Me? I simply did what was required, obeyed orders from above, passed them on," he answered. "Some of it was all right. Some a bit harrowing, especially the Slapton Sands affair."

"Slapton Sands?" She frowned. "Oh yes, I know what you mean. In early 1944. It was all hushed up, wasn't it? We never knew much about it until a few years ago, even though Withyford isn't all that far away. I suppose it was kept under wraps according to the thirty year rule. Then there was some BBC programme about it."

"Yes. It was the most appalling disaster. It makes one wonder just how much information was withheld by the authorities. I happened to be involved because I was stationed at Dartmouth, liaising with your Navy, so I was one of the American officers who saw things first hand. I knew all about those poor devils, my countrymen, who were on a rehearsal for D-Day. The German intelligence got wind of it. There were about a thousand casualties altogether, mostly drowned. But I suppose the Chiefs of Staff thought, quite rightly, that it would be criminal to send troops to land on enemy occupied territory without any experience, and that part of the Devon coast is amazingly similar to Normandy. But can you imagine it? An area of thirty thousand acres having to be evacuated. Families required to move out of their homes and be rehoused. Farmers having to be compensated for abandoned crops, stock having to be sold. It must have been heartbreaking for local residents."

"I imagine they must have known what it was all in aid of?"

"Yes. But, incredibly, not much leaked out about the failure of the exercise. Everyone was sworn to secrecy. It took me quite a while to come to terms with it. It was one of those tragedies of the war I wanted to blot out at the time."

"It must have made it all the more difficult for you when the invasion did take place."

"Well, it wasn't easy for anyone. Actually, though, in the event, we lost less men during the initial landings than at Slapton Sands. Of course, it must have been so much worse for those in command. Eisenhower, for instance. Did you know he wrote two communiques before the Second Front started? One for failure, one for success. If it had been the former he said that the responsibility would be his and his alone. I always felt proud of him for that. The bad weather held up the whole operation for twenty-four hours. Then I suppose he couldn't keep 200,000 men cooped up waiting any longer and was simply obliged to say, 'Let's go'!"

Rex became silent for a while, remembering. "I thought of you, Anna," he went on, "as we crossed the Channel and then, a little later on, when I heard that Hitler had targeted his V1 and V2 rockets on London from the *Pas de Calais*, I prayed they wouldn't hit St Thomas's and you'd be all right."

She was mortified. "Rex," she said, quietly, "I wasn't there then. I'd been sent to this place near Staines, the other hospital."

"For how long?"

"Quite a while."

"What did they do to you?"

She knew she would have to tell him now. That it couldn't be avoided any longer. "They put me to sleep, or tried to, for three weeks. There was this Austrian doctor, a Jewish refugee called

Hertz, who was pioneering this kind of treatment for stress, but mostly for servicemen. I felt so inadequate, such a failure, especially with the Second Front starting and not pulling my weight."

"Were you helped by the treatment?"

"Not really. It wasn't Dr Hertz's fault. He tried, but the drugs didn't suit me. And they affected my memory for some time afterwards. I came back here. My mother was concerned, but unable to understand. My father was more sympathetic. We used to go for long walks. We came up here sometimes. I can recall him once saying, 'That young man, Rex Harman, you still think of him, I expect?' And when I answered, 'Yes,' he asked, 'Do you know where he is?' After I replied, 'I've no idea,' my father said, 'I'm so sorry for you, my dear.' You were the one person I remembered perfectly clearly."

"Did you go back to St Thomas's?"

"No. Shortly after that my father became ill. He'd never been very strong, but I didn't know he had a weak heart until near the end. I wasn't passed fit enough to go on with my training and there seemed a ready-made job for me at home. I was glad to be able to nurse him, not to feel entirely useless. My mother wasn't cut out for that sort of thing. He died just before the end of the war. I hated being alone with my mother, but I couldn't leave her just then. I had an idea of doing private nursing sometime. One didn't have to be fully trained and I felt it was all I was fit for. Besides, there would be periods when I could come home and keep my mother company, wherever she happened to be. It was obvious she wouldn't be able to remain at the rectory, or that any new incumbent would live there either. It was too large and so cold and dilapidated."

Anna's revelations had distressed Rex. He changed the subject, although hardly to an easier one. "This Mallinder chap," he said. "Did he get in touch with you at once after VE Day?"

"Oh, yes. His parents weren't at all pleased, as you can imagine. He landed at Dover and came straight to Withyford instead of going up to Yorkshire. Of course, my mother was delighted. After all the privations and difficulties of running the rectory in wartime, dealing with evacuees and billetees and then my illness and my father's death, I think she saw Dick as some kind of saviour — a future titled son-in-law who would take care of us both."

"And how did you see him?"

"Older. Desperately thin. Going bald. He had a huge lump on his forehead where he had walked into an anti-tank trap in Brussels twenty-four hours earlier, having been wined and dined a little too enthusiastically by some Belgians the night before. I felt . . . terribly sorry for him."

"So pity was akin to love?"

"If you put it like that."

"It's getting colder," Rex said, linking an arm through hers. "I think we should go back."

They walked down the grass track into the village. The rectory, flanked by two enormous golden-leaved beech trees, looked well cared-for as they drew nearer. There was someone clipping the hedge in front, a woman of about forty, secateurs in hand, intent on her job. But as they passed, she looked up and smiled at them. A nice person, Anna felt, somehow welcoming, even though she couldn't have known them from Adam.

On an impulse, Anna came forward and said, "Forgive me for what must seem nosiness. But I used to live here."

The woman's eyes widened. She was pretty in a plump, pink and white, rather innocent way. "Oh, *really*? Do come in. Please. I'd love to have an excuse to break off."

It was impossible to refuse her obviously sincere invitation. Having introduced Rex and discovered that the present owner was called Jane Everett, Anna said, "My maiden name was Linsdale. My father was rector here for many years, until almost the end of the war, in fact."

"Goodness," Jane Everett replied, "I'd love to hear what it was like then. We only came here a little while ago. I gather the house has changed hands quite a few times since the '40s. I do hope it won't seem too upsetting for you, coming back."

"Not at all. It's lovely to find it looking so cherished," Anna replied, as she and Rex were ushered into a room which bore no resemblance to the heavily-furnished, gloomy, antimacassared one she remembered. This one was light and airy, full of yellows and greens, with big french windows opening on to a wide grass path, with herbaceous borders on either side. "You've improved the place beyond all recognition," Anna continued, once they were seated and had accepted the drinks which Jane Everett insisted on giving them.

"It's nice of you to say so," she answered. "But it isn't all due to us. We've only been here since the end of the '80s. We haven't done all that much, except, perhaps, in the garden. I'm a keen but very amateur gardener. The whole place seemed exactly right for us. I've always wanted to live in the country. John, my husband, is, alas, away on business quite a lot, but I have our twins, Rose and Belinda, for company. They're able to go to a good day school near here, which will take them right through until they're eighteen. I've a horror of boarding-schools, I'm afraid."

Someone after my own heart, Anna thought, as Jane Everett went on, cheerfully, "We're hoping to install a swimming-pool next year. It'll mean forgoing a chunk of the kitchen garden, but I think the need for that kind of recreation has taken priority over fresh vegetables. Not that we'll exactly go short of them. There's always been a surplus."

Anna thought of her mother, struggling to put the flower borders down to Brussels sprouts in the war, or trying to make every inch of the rectory garden productive. She felt a twinge of guilt. It must have been hell, surely, married to a saint, trying to cope with a potentially flighty daughter, living a life for which she was not cut out. Why *had* Janet Linsdale let herself in for it? What on earth would she have said about a *swimming-pool* at the rectory? Rank hedonism? Anna seemed to recall a few dips in the river during her youth, cold and full of weeds. Only later on, at boarding-school, had she learnt to swim — and never very efficiently, at that.

"Look," she heard Janet Everett now saying, "seeing that the rectory must hold so many memories for you, supposing you both come to dinner at the weekend, when my husband will be home?"

"I'm afraid we shall be gone by then," Anna said, quickly.

"Oh dear, too bad. But if you wouldn't find me too dull by myself, how about lunch on Thursday?"

7

BACK for lunch at the Withyford Arms that day, the girl whom Anna felt was a descendant of the Shergold family, waited on them again. She had evidently checked up on the hotel's new guests, for although she had hitherto addressed them perfectly politely as 'sir' or 'madam', at the end of the meal, to Anna's surprise, she asked, "Would you like coffee in the lounge, Lady Mallinder?" Seeing Rex nod, Anna replied, "Yes, please," and then she was suddenly emboldened to remark, "Forgive me, but you remind me so much of someone of about my age whom I knew in my youth, a Della Shergold. Are you, by any chance, related?"

The girl stared at her. "Why, yes. She's my Gran. Mum's mother. She married a Fred Hapgood."

Anna was quick to notice that she spoke of Della in the present tense. "She's still alive, then?"

"Yes. Lives up on Downside in one of them old folks' places. You know, there's a warden and what have you. Mum wanted her to live with us, but she wouldn't have it. They . . . don't get on, even though Mum's been ever so good to her. You're from these parts, then?"

"Yes. My maiden name was Linsdale. I used to live at the rectory."

"You was the rector's daughter?"

"Yes."

"My Gran looks a lot older than you."

Anna smiled. The innocent spontaneous remark seemed entirely sincere. "Do you think your grandmother would like me to visit her?"

The girl hesitated. "She might and she mightn't. It depends if she takes to you. Sometimes she's O.K. Sometimes she gives everyone short shrift. My name's Madge. Madge Musselwhite. You might remember my Dad's family, too."

"Indeed I do." So long ago. The Shergolds, the Hapgoods and the Musselwhites. Names which Anna had scarcely thought of for many years.

Now, their owners came back to her extraordinarily clearly. She could recall their faces, their idiosyncracies, especially the Shergolds' with their 'fallen' daughter, Della.

"Did your grandmother have any other children?" Anna asked, and sensed that Madge seemed slightly embarrassed.

"She had two other kids, two boys, much younger than my Mum."

It all fitted in. Della had produced an illegitimate daughter, Madge's Mum, and then one of the Hapgood sons had evidently made an honest woman of her. It explained why Della had never taken to her eldest child, why her granddaughter seemed a little chary about revealing any more family history.

"Perhaps," Anna said, "I might chance my luck. Go and see her and ask if she remembers me."

To her surprise, Madge answered, "I could take you, if you like, when we're finished here. It's fairly quiet today."

Anna looked at Rex enquiringly. It would not be altogether his scene and he was quick to appreciate the fact. "You go ahead," he said. "I'd like to drive into Dorchester. I've got an idea for tomorrow. I need a few local maps."

Shortly before three, Anna and Madge set off for Downside. Anna realised that the girl must know about her grandmother's history. One couldn't keep a thing like that quiet in a small village community. She could see Della's American corporal as if it were yesterday. Fat, a real doughboy, as they were called. She wondered what had happened to him. Was he killed in the war? Did he know about Della and conveniently get posted? Or was he now an old man in the States with no knowledge of the daughter he had sired or the granddaughter who was now walking beside her? Anna recalled having overheard Miss Maidment once telling her mother that Della's seducer had hailed from Tennessee. It was odd how such a snippet of information had stuck in her mind. She remembered how the censorious old spinster had managed to make even the name of his homeground seem somehow sinful.

Turning into Parson's Lane they passed the new red-brick rectory, where two grubby children were playing outside, a small supermarket next door and the place which used to be the village school but was now, Madge informed her, a community centre. "The kids all go to Dorchester by bus," she remarked. "It's not the same. Gran's got a book of old photos of Withyford. If she's in a good mood she might show it to you. I dare say it would bring back a few memories. I'm not sure but wot your dad isn't in it. Ever so nice, he looked. Not like the present rector, all beard and glasses."

"Do you go to church?" Anna asked, hoping that it would not be too dark to call there on her return journey. It was something she and Rex would have done earlier, had they not been waylaid so agreeably by Jane Everett. Her conscience had begun to trouble her that she had been so negligent over the years about visiting her father's grave, how stark the white marble tombstone had last seemed, with its marble surrounds filled with white granite chippings, how her mother had insisted that this was by far the best and easiest solution to the problem of upkeep. 'It's what he would have wished, Anna,' Janet Linsdale had said, although her daughter had not been so sure. Yet she realised that her mother, knowing that she would probably be leaving Withyford and quite unable to deal with any grass-trimming or fresh flowers, had been perfectly right from the practical point of view. Janet had made everything extraordinarily simple and when she herself, having gone to live with a female cousin in Halifax, died many years after her husband, Anna found that she was both shocked yet grateful to read her mother's short explicit funeral instructions: *As I do not believe in life after death. I wish my body to be cremated at the nearest crematorium with the least possible fuss.*

Had Janet never believed in the hereafter, Anna had wondered. All that church-going, all those parish duties of a rector's wife. Had her whole life been a sham? Why on earth had she married Robert Linsdale? Surely her attitude must have been similar to that of Madge Musselwhite, considering what the girl was now telling her.

"I don't go to church. There's not many as do. The rector here holds a service every three weeks. He's got two other parishes to look after. It's pathetic, really. The place is only used for weddings and funerals. The chap I'm living with says we'll just get hitched in a register office when the time comes. Though, in a way, I'd like a proper wedding. I saw some smashing wedding dresses in a shop in Dorchester the other day."

In spite of her awareness of present trends, Anna could not help being dismayed. She knew this sort of thing happened all the time, that Chloe might well be doing the same as Madge in a few years, that she might easily have the same outlook, but Anna was old-fashioned and romantic enough to wish it were not now the way of the world. For a girl to cohabit with a man and then, one day, calmly dress up in virginal white and go to church to have their union blessed, seemed somehow both hypocritical and brazen. Anna realised, sadly, that it was the childlike desire to dress up that was the main thing Madge did not want to be done out of, if her husband-to-be persisted with his idea of a register office wedding.

"Where are you living?" she asked the girl.

"Caravan," came the cheerful reply. "Permanent site." She waved a hand vaguely in a westerly direction. "Not much to keep clean. Very convenient. Both of us out working every day. My boyfriend's with an electrical engineering firm in Dorchester. Drives a motorbike. You won't say anything to Gran about all this, will you? She'd have a stroke if she knew I wasn't still living with Mum."

"No," Anna replied, slowing down slightly as they started the steep climb up to Downside, accepting the fact that Della would obviously be appalled if she knew that her granddaughter was, as she would call it, living in sin. She had probably never been able to come to terms with her own 'sin', even though it had never included actual cohabiting. Hence her dislike of the evidence of, maybe, a single lapse on a summer evening resulting in the birth of Madge's mother. They were nearing Della's home now and Anna was amazed that the authorities had chosen to build old people's accommodation in such a high inconvenient spot. It was strange what bureaucratic minds seemed to think up these days.

Outside Number 24 there was a small paved area and a tub of evergreen by the front porch. To the left, there was a window behind which a curtain twitched.

Madge rang the bell and presently what Anna could only think of as an apparition peered round the door, which had been carefully latched on the inside by a chain.

"Yus?" The voice was deep, husky.

"It's me, Gran. Madge. I've brought you a visitor."

"Who is it?" Half a face, some straggly white hair and one glittering eye looked at them suspiciously.

"Someone you used to know, Gran. The rector's daughter. Way back. When you was both young."

There was a fumbling with the chain and presently the door opened to reveal the full extent of the ravages which time had wrought on Della Hapgood, nee Shergold.

"What do you want, then?" The old

woman stared at Anna. She did not ask them in.

Anna began to wish she had not come. This ancient crone — for Anna could only think of her as such — must only be a few years older than herself. She remained glowering at them, resentfully. "I thought . . . I'd like to see you again, Della," she said, almost apologetically. "I . . . we . . . knew each other in the war." As soon as she mentioned war, Anna realised that she had made a gaffe.

"War?" Della Hapgood spat out the word. "Why would I want to remember that?"

"But Gran," Madge broke in, "you always said as how the rector was so good to you then. You've got a book with his picture in. I'm sure," she went on, trying to bring more tact into a difficult situation than Anna would have credited her with, "that Lady Mallinder would like to see it."

Perhaps the fact that her visitor was titled had something to do with it, for Della's attitude changed a little. "All right," she answered, though still grudgingly.

She led them into a small room, clean, warm, but cluttered. Every available ledge or furniture top was covered by knick-knacks or memorabilia of one sort or another although, oddly enough, few photographs. There was no fireplace. A tiny black and white television set appeared to be the focal point. There were three chairs, one easy one which was obviously Della's and two upright ones in which Madge and Anna now sat. Della still continued to stare at her, disconcertingly.

"Taken you a long time to come back," she remarked, at length.

"Yes. I'm afraid it has." Anna felt she was at a complete disadvantage and wondered how soon she could reasonably make a departure.

"Can I show Lady Mallinder your photo book, Gran?" Madge said. Of the three of them, she seemed by far the most at ease.

"You can get it if you like." Della jerked her head in the direction of a small cupboard.

Madge did as she was bidden, and Anna dutifully began to turn the pages.

At the beginning there was one with a caption underneath: *Sunday at Withyford, 1922.* The year she was born. She could see the church and people coming out of it, a man in a surplice shaking hands. Her father must have had quite a good congregation in those days. A little further on she came across a photograph of both her parents taken, it would seem, at some kind of fête. Her father looked incredibly young and handsome; her mother was wearing some shapeless garment with a cloche hat pulled well down over her face which, even then, appeared to be scowling slightly.

In the centre of the book there was a double-page spread of the village school. "My Ernie and Albert are sitting in the front row," Della suddenly remarked. "And Mum's at the back," Madge chipped in. The old woman in front of them said nothing. It was plain to Anna that although she might have been forced to accept her only daughter physically, she had rejected her mentally from birth.

"What is your mother's Christian name?" Anna asked Madge, gently, feeling unaccountably saddened and angry with Della. She was taken aback when again Della broke in, "The rector, your dad, said Gladys was a nice name. 'Twere all the same to me. I were that ill after she were born."

"I'm sorry," Anna replied, hypocritically, wondering, but not liking to ask, the nature of her illness. She turned over the rest of the pages quickly. The light was beginning to fade outside and she stood up. "It's been nice seeing you again, Della," she said, knowing that she did not mean it and that Della herself probably also knew. She and Madge made their way out of the front door. It had not been a pleasant experience.

On the way down to the village, she asked Madge exactly how ill her grandmother had been after the birth of her mother. The girl did not reply at once. Then she said, "Well, she went a bit queer, if you ask me, although Mum's always stuck up for her and says it was what they now call post-natal depression." After a moment or two, she continued, "Well, you obviously know the story. Mum wasn't wanted and I'm sure you know why."

8

THE church was locked. Anna had been afraid that it would be. Gone were the days when a place of worship freely welcomed all and sundry, when no one rifled collection boxes, stole vestments from the vestry, desecrated the consecrated.

But it was not really the interior she wanted to see. It was a corner on the east side of the graveyard, a place beside which, forty-seven years earlier, she had stood watching as her father's coffin was lowered into its grave, a grave by which she now stood, shivering slightly, in the half light of a cold October evening. She remembered the bishop's sombre words: *Earth to earth, ashes to ashes, dust to dust, in the sure and certain hope of the resurrection to eternal life.* It was nice of him to have conducted the funeral service himself, she felt, a fitting tribute to the saintly man her father had been.

Only the headstone and surrounds of

his grave now remained. The white chippings had given way to grass and moss. On the headstone she could just discern: *In loving memory of Robert Linsdale, 1892 – 1945 rector of this parish, R.I.P.* How young he had been to die. She wished she could believe in eternal life, that her father was up there in heaven looking down on her now, glad that she had come.

The yew tree which stood sentinel beside the grave seemed overpowering, even menacing. The evening was closing in. She was filled with sadness, remorse. Why did I never get to know him better? Could it have been because of my mother? Her jealousy? No, I must not take refuge in that. And why have I not come here before? Arranged for the better upkeep of his grave, instead of accepting my mother's 'easiest solution' which meant there was no need. Uncertain, confused, she sent up a small prayer asking for forgiveness.

There was a step behind her and she turned, startled. A youngish man, casually dressed in jeans and anorak, said, "I saw you turn in here just now," and for a moment she panicked: Oh God, no. No one is safe these days. Could you be a potential rapist, even though I'm as old as Methuselah?

"I'm the rector here," he went on, putting at least some of her fears to rest.

"Really?" Her voice sounded unnaturally high, still frightened, until she realised she should have known. He was Madge's 'all beard and glasses' man, all right.

"Yes. I'm the latest in a line of several recent incumbents. There's a quick turnover. We live in — that small redbrick ghastly edifice which you may have noticed along Parson's Way."

"Well, yes," she answered. "I was told that was your house."

"Something of a comedown," he went on, "when you compare it to the old rectory where the Everetts now live."

Anna hesitated. She thought it might be best to get back to the hotel. Rex could be waiting. Then she decided, for politeness sake, to remark, "I used to live there once, too, back in the war."

He stared at her as if she might have been a visitor from outer space.

"*Really*," he said, "you were the Reverend Linsdale's daughter," adding, rather as Jane Everett had done, but with almost childlike interest and awe, "what was it like then?"

"Then?" she laughed. "Well, not at all like it is now. Mrs Everett showed it to me . . . to us . . . this morning. It's quite different. It's been made much better. Much more beautiful."

"I suppose so. Nice people, the Everetts. I'm glad that your old home is being so well looked after. Would you care to see my humbler abode?"

She wished he wouldn't sound quite so Uriah Heepish.

Looking at her watch, she replied, "Thank you, but I think I should be getting back to the Withyford Arms where we're staying."

"Ah, but perhaps now that you've found us again, you might come some other time."

"Well, yes. I was wondering . . . if I were to send you a cheque towards the church funds, could I possibly add something extra to be used specifically to cover the cost of restoring my father's grave and keeping it in good order?"

"But, *of course*! How kind, how very kind. I would be only too happy . . . "

Another figure suddenly loomed out of the darkness and came towards them. To her relief, she saw it was Rex.

"I guessed you might be here," he said. "I thought if I came this way I could hardly miss you."

She tried to introduce the two men but realised she did not know the name of the rector. But, surprisingly, he now seemed equal to the occasion, for he put out a hand and said, rather as Americans were apt to do, "Coren. Patrick Coren. Your wife tells me she was brought up at the old rectory."

They did not disillusion him. It seemed too complicated, unnecessary, not that they felt that Patrick Coren would have been in any way shocked. He must have become inured to unconventional relationships by now. Besides, she and Rex were simply old friends, weren't they? Anna thought of the many more flagrant liaisons there must be on his doorstep. Madge and her boyfriend, for instance.

Walking back to the Withyford Arms, Rex put his arm through hers and said, "I wish you were."

"What?"

"I wish you were what the rector assumed you were — my wife."

She flushed, glad that the darkness prevented him from noticing. He had intimated that their little holiday would be perfectly platonic. Separate rooms and all that. Suddenly she was not so sure. She liked him so much. She was so pleased he had come back into her life, that they were putting the record straight. But marriage, sex? She had given up thinking about that a long time ago, at least, in connection with herself. The passionate girl she had once been had gone for ever. Sometimes, she thought, wryly, she could hardly recognise her. When one got to a certain age, the desire for a physical relationship seemed to leave one. Or, at any rate, it had left her. She knew that it generally lasted much longer with men than women, and that there was a vast difference in the way various women felt about it. But for herself, she simply seemed detached from that side of life. Could it be that her unfortunate marriage had something to do with it?

Occasionally, she would look at the gossip columns with astonishment, read how some man had left some wife or vice versa, how some woman was now on her third or fourth or maybe fifth marriage, how some affair had ended and another was beginning. It was really all to do with sex, wasn't it? Not love. And the poor bewildered children, the result of all these shenanigans, were dragged around from pillar to post, all because of this strange, presumably uncontrollable, urge which the good Lord had ordained to make the world go round.

They were nearing the Withyford Arms now. Rex turned his face towards her and in the light of the street lamp she saw his expression: infinitely kind, comforting, even flattering. Quietly, she said, "Oh, Rex, it's so good to be with you. But have you forgotten? I'm a grandmother, old. I wouldn't make a good wife for anyone."

"I didn't mention *anyone*, Anna." There was no mistaking what he meant.

Once inside the hotel she left him quickly and went up to her room, afraid that she was going to cry. She realised that Rex had rekindled an emotion rather different from the last one she had experienced with him. It had nothing to do with sex or marriage. Could it be love?

That night at dinner they were both quiet, gentle with each other. Madge appeared to be off duty and they were waited on by a young man with an earring in one ear and spiky hair. Anna asked Rex if he had found the maps he wanted and he said, "Yes, if you don't think it would be too far . . . "

"You want to go to Slapton Sands," she filled in for him.

The empathy was there. She knew exactly what he wanted to do without having to be told.

"Quite right," he replied. "It may seem a bit ghoulish, but I'd like to see the place again. I gather a monument's been put up, a monument to the living, a kind of thank-you from the Americans to all those poor people who had to evacuate their homes in order to make it possible for us to practise for D-Day, even though one of those exercises did end in such disaster."

"I'd love to go, Rex," she answered. "You're telling me things about my own country that I hardly knew."

9

FOR the second time in less than twenty-four hours, Anna found herself looking at words of remembrance. She stood beside Rex on the sands at Slapton — sands of silence as they were once termed — and read:

This memorial has been presented by the U.S. Army authorities to the people of South Hams, who generously left their homes and their lands to provide a battle practice area for the successful assault on Normandy in June 1944. Their action resulted in the saving of hundreds of lives and contributed in no small measure to the success of the operation.

"But many American lives were lost here," she said, sadly.

"Yes," he answered. "But I suppose it was thought this was the best, the kindest way to record what happened rather than mention the disaster."

"Were many of your men picked up?"

"Some. And some by the Germans. They referred to them as 'swimming soldiers captured'. Our wounded were taken to a military hospital station at Sherborne. The authorities there were told not to ask questions."

She shivered a little, as she had done at her father's graveside, and Rex immediately insisted that they must get back to the car. On one side of them lay the English Channel, deceptively calm, on the other lay the land which had once, a long time ago, been changed into a mock battlefield and for a long time after that had lain still and lonely, waiting for the life it had once known to reestablish itself.

"Do you think," she said, as they got into the car and started to eat the picnic which the Withyford Arms had put up for them, "that there are many people living here now who can remember being evacuated?"

"Not many, I would have thought. Possibly a few of our age or younger. But everyone moves around so these days. They don't seem to remain on their homeground for long. Nor do they come back to look at it all that much, unless they have relatives or are sentimental old things like you and me. You realise, don't you, that this car park where we're sitting is on the site of what was once the Royal Sands Hotel. Seven and sixpence a night I believe it used to cost in 1939."

"What happened to it? Did it get shelled?"

"Well, it was evacuated right early on in the war, being so much on the sea front. Then some farmer's dog, name of Pincher I believe, set off a mine close by. I think he escaped but half the building was demolished, so it already had a kind of war-torn look before we got here. I suppose it was eventually pulled down and never rebuilt."

"Where were you when the exercise was going on?"

"I was meant to be liaising between our headquarters at Dittisham and Okehampton, which was supposed to be an imaginary Cherbourg. It was not a particularly creditworthy role, especially when I think how lack of co-ordination was at the root of our troubles, that and the fact that one of our ships holed a sister ship. Of course, don't forget there was more than one exercise, but Operation Tiger was the one which failed so abysmally. The German E-boats slipped out of Cherbourg and gave us hell."

"But surely, with all that naval activity in the Channel, the Allied Command must have realised that the enemy was bound to detect a lot of what was going on."

"Yes. But I suppose they hoped that the frequent massing of invasion craft, which were later dispersed, would confuse the Germans as to where the Second Front would start. But you know, Anna, looking back, I can't believe how we won. Sometimes I even wonder whether it all really happened."

"When did you get back to the States?"

"Not till '46. But I wasn't in a hurry. I had nothing to go back for. I heard about your marriage, oddly enough, from a chap called Eccles who'd flown out from England to Luneburg, where the armistice was signed. For some unknown reason, I'd been made a Colonel by then and was on Ike's staff. Eccles happened to know your husband. They'd been prisoners-of-war together, only Eccles had managed to escape early on. Dressed up as a nun and made it all through Germany and France and over the Pyrenees. We got talking and he told me what things were like back in England, how so many P.O.W.s were getting married to girls they'd only just met, but a friend, Dick Mallinder, had just got married to a girl who had 'waited'. Your name cropped up as being one of the faithful types who had never sent a rejection slip."

"I see."

Haltingly, she tried to explain to him the pressure, the pleasure her mother had shown at Dick Mallinder's return and his obvious desire to marry her daughter as soon as possible. She described her feeling of inability to turn him down after all he had been through, the way he had talked, non-stop, about his experiences and his gratitude that so much happiness now awaited him.

"I was completely taken over," she said. "I know it sounds feeble, but that is honestly what happened. Dick's family seemed just as keen as my mother. They were insistent that the wedding should take place in Yorkshire, not Withyford. They made the excuse that it was the least they could do, my father having died so recently, and I believe my mother was secretly delighted. We were given the treatment, all the trappings which the landed gentry could muster up in an England exhausted by six years of war. There had certainly been plenty of champagne from Sir Reginald Mallinder's cellars, which had been carefully put aside for this very event. Ten of Dick's P.O.W. friends formed a guard of honour outside the church and, having imbibed a little too freely at lunch, they seemed to sway slightly as we walked underneath.

"Where did you go on honeymoon?"

"Scarborough. After we set off I realised that Dick was in no state to drive, so we swapped places and I took the wheel. It had been terribly difficult to find accommodation anywhere at that time, because England was overflowing with returning servicemen, particularly Americans, waiting to go home. But my mother-in-law, who seemed to have boundless capacity for pulling strings in every direction, got us into a hotel, thanks to a friend of a friend."

"Weren't you mortified at having to drive there?"

"Well, I think I simply felt sorry, not just for myself, but for Dick and all his friends who, through no fault of their own, had been forced to waste some of the best years of their lives shut up in appalling conditions. Dick had already told me that, at one point, he had been so hungry that he had exchanged a dead mouse for another man's orange peel. So it was small wonder that all the P.O.W.s were warned against overeating or drinking too much on repatriation. It wasn't surprising, either, that the warning was desperately hard to heed. Poor Dick seemed to find it impossible."

"Always?"

"Off and on. I tried to do all I could. You know, to help, to understand. I mean, that's what a nurse's training is mostly for, isn't it? Yesterday, when you said about pity being akin to love, I realised how right you were."

"Were you ever happy together? I

mean, forgive my asking, but what happened on the honeymoon?"

"Oh, that was a complete disaster. We arrived back at the Dower House with the marriage still unconsummated. We were meant to live there until Dick felt ready to take on the estate. His father had already intimated that he would like to retire and that we should then swop homes. 'As soon as you feel the time has come,' he said to Dick. The trouble was that that time never seemed to arrive."

"Because of the drink?"

"Yes. Sometimes I thought I . . . we were winning. When I became pregnant with Steven I really began to have hope, I so desperately wanted a child. But as soon as he was born, Dick had a relapse and I wasn't able to keep the trouble from my in-laws or my mother any longer. She had gone to live with a female cousin in Halifax and I think she sensed the situation before the Mallinders, even though they were practically on our doorstep. Sometimes, I used to think that if we'd been on our own, further away from them all, it might have been better. But, looking back, it might have been worse. I mean, at least Dick had the constant fear that one or the other of them would turn up suddenly when . . . he was not at his best."

"I suppose your mother was disappointed."

"Yes. Although I still think my marrying into a titled family compensated for a lot. When my father-in-law died suddenly from a stroke and we moved into the Hall and I became Lady Mallinder it meant no end to her."

"But what happened? How could your husband cope?"

"Well, Dick went to one of those places for a cure before we actually got installed in the big house. When he came back I really did think he'd beaten the trouble and for a time all went well. Money didn't seem to be a problem. We had a nanny and a new young agent called Andrew Chandler. Then one day, I forget, about two or three years later, Andrew mentioned to me something about being worried that Dick wanted to sell off some land. I couldn't imagine why and said so. Andrew got a bit embarrassed, but I dragged it out of him. The estate had gone into the red. I found out that Dick had been gambling quite heavily in an effort to recoup."

"Oh, God, Anna." He put a hand over hers and she did not withdraw it. She only said, "Don't you think that's quite enough about me for now. How about going and looking at that tank at Tor Cross which you've heard was rescued from the sea?"

10

THEY spent the afternoon driving slowly to this point and that: the various villages he so well remembered in their army-occupied days; a new nature reserve; the tank brought up from the sea thanks to the dedicated efforts of someone on whom, like Rex, the tragedy of Slapton Sands had made such a deep impression; the little churches whose treasures had long been reinstated. "They had to be so careful with them," Rex recalled. "I remember the authorities saying the old chancel screens were as brittle as gingerbread."

They sat in a small café having a cup of tea before their return journey. "It's all so peaceful now," he kept repeating, "as if none of it had ever happened. I suppose all wars are a kind of aberration, a departure from the norm and then life, ordinary life, goes on its way again. Perhaps the world has to have a shake-up now and then, but, looking back, I'm glad I never had children." He stopped, suddenly. "Oh Anna, forgive me." She had told him briefly of the tragedy which had resulted in her taking on the responsibility for Chloe's upbringing. So far she had not wished to enlarge on it.

This time it was she who put out a hand of comfort. "Tell me," she said, quietly, "what happened to you at the end of the war?"

A look of anguish crossed his face and he began his story with difficulty. "I simply took what was going when it came to the opposite sex," he said, "if you don't mind my putting it so crudely. I'd made no other serious attachments after you. I felt a great desire to settle down, but I knew if I wanted to marry I'd have to get myself a worthwhile job and in that respect I was lucky. One thing about the army is that you do come up against a lot of different people and you do make certain friends. One of mine happened to be the son of a rich Chicago family who owned a hell of a lot of real estate. This chap, Seymour McCutcheon, had a kind of ready-made job to go back to, but I guess he needed help, a sort of agent. I had no experience of that kind of business but I suppose by now Seymour reckoned I had a few administrative skills, having been a colonel on Ike's staff. Anyhow, he got in touch with me when I eventually went back to the States. He was younger than I was. There was probably a bit of hero-worship in our relationship. God knows I didn't deserve it, but he asked his father to take me on. Said we worked well together. I came in by the back door, so to speak."

"And made a success of it."

"Success? Anna, what *is* success? I was able to manage the estate all right. It seemed child's play after what I'd been doing. But I made a mess of my private life."

"How do you mean?"

"I married my friend's sister."

"Was that such a terrible thing to do?"

"No, not really, I suppose. Seymour thought it a splendid idea and his family was perfectly agreeable. I'd buckled to and worked hard and I think they thought I'd be a good influence on Ros, help to calm her down. She was a bit of a wild one. Not beautiful like you, but nervy, high spirited, the kind of girl who would get up on tables at parties and dance barefoot. That kind of thing. I admit I was attracted in the beginning. I suppose I'd become a bit too serious one way and another, what with my disappointment over you and the war itself and having witnessed some of the horrors of the concentration camps. I don't want to go into that, Anna, ever. In 1946 I truly wanted to forget, and Ros McCutcheon seemed an excellent companion to help me to do so. We had what I dare say you'd call over here a society wedding. A bit like yours, I suppose. I'm afraid we Americans are even more snobbish than you when it comes to that kind of thing. The McCutcheons gave us a slap-up do, inviting all the smart set, as it was referred to, of Chicago. My parents travelled from Idaho, where they had a smallish farm. I know they felt sadly out of place, besides thinking I was making a big mistake. How right they were.

"Things went O.K.," he continued, "for a while. No kids came along, although I believe at that time I was still young and optimistic enough to have welcomed them. I'm sure my in-laws would. Ros didn't seem bothered one way or the other, but I have a feeling she wouldn't have cared for her social life to be curtailed. Sometimes, when I had to work late and couldn't make some engagement, she'd go alone. There were always plenty of guys willing to escort her home, although I don't think she was ever actually unfaithful. It was simply a good time she was after and she blamed me for not giving it to her. It wasn't sex but attention, she needed, even demanded. I suppose we might have become divorced if she hadn't become ill. She collapsed on the dance floor one night when I'd taken her out in an effort to make amends for what she called my 'neglect'. I thought it was only a temporary indisposition, that she'd been doing too much, but the doctor ordered her into hospital for some tests. To cut a long story short, it was the beginning of muscular dystrophy."

"Oh, *no*!" They were both silent for a while and then Anna asked, "Was she told?"

"Not then. I . . . we kept it from her

as long as we could. We were afraid she wouldn't be able to take it. When the illness progressed and she did find out, she became aggressive, abusive even and, I'm afraid, horribly possessive. With no suitors dancing attendance on her any more and being stuck at home, she felt trapped. It was then she found your photo one day. She blamed what she called my 'lack of desire' on my love for you. She could have been right, I suppose, although I'm no saint, Anna. I've never been exactly . . . celibate. But when illness struck Ros, I tried to put all my energies, as far as possible, into work and looking after her as well as I could."

"And then?" Anna felt it was vital to keep Rex talking now that he had told her so much.

"Well, then, Anna, Ros's illness just went on and on. Everyone, her parents, her brother — Seymour had married by then — and even the doctors expected her to die. But she didn't. Before she became too incapacitated, I'd take her on holiday or suggest an evening out. I had to be careful, though, where we went. On one occasion there happened to be a dance floor and she insisted I escorted her round it, even though she was dragging her feet and I more or less had to hold her up. Eventually, of course, it was a question of nurses and a wheel-chair. Her parents were very good — to both of us. Ros's father left money in trust for her in his will. Then it came to me. Sometimes I don't feel entitled to it."

"But you did your best. Looked after Ros till the end. Looked after the business. What more could you have done?"

He was silent. Then he said, "I should never have married her, Anna. I suppose I went along with it all rather as you did. I completely understand what happened to you in '45 and why. We both made mistakes. If only we had gotten together back in '43. We've no one to blame but ourselves. Me much more than you." He gave her a rueful smile. "Although I reckon that old busybody, Lizzie Maidment, had a lot to answer for."

She laughed. He paid their bill and they got up to go. It was quite dark and, once again, they said little on the way back to Withyford, although by now Rex seemed completely at home with left-hand driving. Usually Anna disliked being driven. With Rex, she had no qualms.

It came to her that they were over half way through their visit to the West Country. Tomorrow they would have lunch with Jane Everett at the rectory. On Friday they would return to London. She would collect Chloe from Atherstone Lodge. What of Rex? He had given no hint as to how long he was intending to stay in England. Their spur of the moment decision to travel into the past was something out of context, completely out of keeping with the staid conventional life she now lived. Aware that Chloe would have been surprised by her message to the school, Anna had sent the child a postcard as soon as she arrived in Withyford. It had, inevitably, been slightly ambiguous. She had simply said that a very old friend had come to visit her — no gender mentioned — whom she had not seen since the last war, and they had decided to tour the West Country for a few days, but she would be back to pick Chloe up on Friday, as usual.

But what would Rex do? He had apparently retained his room at the Hilton, but he had made no mention of any other plans. Were there more places he wanted to see? Would he want her to accompany him? Suddenly, the thought of parting again seemed heart-breaking. Where would this strange reunion end? They both lived miles apart, half a world away, in fact. He had shown her photographs of a lovely house and a model farmstead in Lake Forest. They both had their respective lives to lead. She with Chloe and her writing and, as for Rex, although he might have retired from looking after the McCutcheon estate, apparently he still worked in an advisory capacity and obviously had quite an establishment of his own to manage, presumably tended by staff in his absence.

He was very quiet at dinner that night and she feared the long drive had tired him. She was totally unprepared for his query when they were sitting in the lounge at about ten o'clock. "It seems silly, doesn't it, Anna," he said, "to say goodnight now, especially as in order to get private bathrooms we both booked a double room. We still have so much to talk about. Would it be such a heinous crime if I shared yours tonight?"

11

IT did not seem a heinous crime. In fact, it seemed perfectly natural. Age did not come into it, nor convention. Rex made love to her slowly, gently, in a way she had never experienced before. In the morning, she realised that she had been wrong in assuming that physical desire had passed her by. She was surprised, but not embarrassed. Their relationship had somehow come into its own. When they decided, before going to lunch at the rectory, to look for the site of the camp where Rex had once been stationed and the Emergency Hospital where she had worked, she felt as if they were a married couple who had been together since youth.

During the past forty-eight hours, Jane Everett had speculated more than once on her unexpected visitors who she had been looking forward to seeing again. Today, she felt even more reason to wonder about them: the tall, good-looking, courteous American and the charming, elegant Englishwoman, who appeared so devoted to each other. She was sure there was 'a story there', as her husband would have remarked; but her natural sensitivity prevented her from asking too many questions. She felt, however, that it was safe to make further enquiries as to what her present home had been like in the '30s and '40s.

"Cold," Anna told her, without hesitation. "There was no central heating and what with food and fuel rationing, my father often had to resort to writing his sermons in the kitchen. It was the only warm place in winter. I was away nursing most of the war, so luckily I only experienced it from time to time. It's lovely to come back to such a *comfortable* home."

"The privations must have made it hard for your parents, especially your mother," Jane said.

"Yes," Anna's voice suddenly lost a little of its cheerfulness. She thought of the already grey-haired Janet, wearing an old thick sweater and shapeless skirt, making some meatless concoction called

Woolton's Pie, named after the food minister; of her mother's valiant efforts in the garden and of how she coped with nit-infested evacuees before their parents swooped down and took them back to London, preferring their children to be subjected to the risk of bombs rather than the rigours of Withyford rectory. It had certainly not been a happy place. The woman in charge made no secret of the fact that she laboured under difficulties. After her mother's death, the cousin with whom she had spent her widowhood, remarked to Anna, 'I fear Janet led a sad life'. And when Anna had asked why she had rarely seemed happy, Cousin Hannah had replied, "My dear, didn't you *know*? She was very much in love with an army officer at the end of the First World War. Believe it or not, your mother was very pretty, very lively in those days."

"Then why ever . . . ?" Anna began, only to be cut short. "The chap was already married," came the laconic answer. "Janet was consumed by guilt. Your father had just been ordained and she was a member of his congregation when she decided to end the affair. I think he helped her in some way and she was grateful to him. But, of course, gratitude is not enough. It turned to resentment after they married and I dare say she felt sexually frustrated.

Anna thought of Rex's assessment of her own reason for marriage, about pity being akin to love. Neither pity nor gratitude, it would appear, could ever be enough. There had to be something else and, looking at him across the table she knew what it was. She and Rex had a relationship based on love, tenderness and sex, which a gap of fifty years had not destroyed. She listened, now, as he talked animatedly to Jane Everett about his own recollections of Withyford in the war, how he had nothing but praise for Anna's father — she noted there was no reference to her mother — and how he considered that the Reverend Robert Linsdale to have been "one of the old school, a really good man. There can't be many of them left, I'm afraid," he said.

Jane Everett shook her head in agreement. "Sadly, no, Pat Coren, our new incumbent, means well, I dare say.

But I have a nasty feeling he's going to try to introduce pop into his services, you know, dancing in the aisles. He's already spoken to me about raking in the younger generation that way. I suppose it's happening everywhere, but I don't want my children catching religion by any of those sort of gimmicks."

Conversation between the three of them went on, easy, relaxed. After lunch, when it was time to go, their hostess begged them to come again. "I know my husband would love to meet you both," she said, and for the first time Anna felt a slight uncertainty, although she promised to keep in touch.

When they got back to the Withyford Arms, as if in answer to her thoughts, Rex came up to her bedroom, took her by the hand and led her across to the spare bed. "You didn't seem too sure about the future, my love," he said, "when you were saying goodbye to Jane Everett." And when Anna remained silent, he went on, "You didn't think, did you, that I was going to let you go a second time? We may not have all that long, Anna, and I don't suppose actual marriage means much to a lot of people these days. But I think it does to you and me. Besides, I believe that granddaughter of yours would prefer our relationship to be regularised. Just think of it, I'll be a step-grandad."

His happy cheerful assumption of the position made her laugh. "If this is a formal proposal," she replied, "then I accept with pleasure. But goodness knows what Chloe will have to say when I tell her about us. I wouldn't like her ever to think too badly of her old grandmother. Deep down, I've a feeling she's quite a conventional little thing. But Rex, you do realise you'd be taking on her as well as me and you've never even met her."

"But that will be put right tomorrow, won't it? I'm looking forward to making her acquaintance. But, please, before I do, won't you tell me a little more about her parents, why you're bringing her up. I don't want to make any gaffes. It's a subject you've avoided so far."

She knew it had to come. She would have to explain, but it wouldn't be easy. It was a story she had never been able to bring herself to tell anyone, except Dr Fenton, and even he only knew the barest details.

"Steven, my son," she began, "was eighteen when Dick died. The estate had been sold some time by then and we'd moved to a small house in Norfolk. It was close to one of those rehabilitation centres. I had a ridiculous hope that, being near at hand, it would give him and, I suppose, me, some kind of moral, if not physical, support. My mother-in-law paid for Steven's schooling. She'd taken herself off to live in a cottage in one of the remoter Yorkshire villages. I don't think she ever wanted to hear about Dick's weakness. She'd always been able to organise people and this was beyond her. We never saw much of her but, when we did, I sensed she blamed me for the situation, that as I'd been a nurse I could have done more to remedy it. As for my own mother, she just gave the appearance of resignation. She'd had enough adversity in her life.

"Dick was quite happy for me to hold the purse strings," Anna went on. "In fact, he asked me to do so. Steven was growing up and was old enough to know what was going on. I think he despised his father and Dick was aware of it. Holidays weren't easy. There was always tension and as soon as Steven passed his A Levels — remarkably well, as it turned out — he didn't go to college as I'd hoped, even though he'd won a scholarship, but pushed off to London."

"Did he get a job?"

"Not at first. I was worried stiff, because it was the so-called swinging sixties. You know, drugs, squats, free love, the lot. But I believe seeing what alcohol had done to his father saved Steven from becoming a drop-out. It wasn't long before he got himself some work on a newspaper. He'd always had plenty of initiative, shown enthusiasm."

"So that must have been a load off your mind."

"Yes. But the trouble was I realised more and more that Dick was failing, if I can use such an old-fashioned word. Sometimes he was quite rambling. He would seem to think he was back in the prisoner-of-war camp. He took to scavenging like he did when he was first repatriated, ticking me off for wasting food. Goodness knows, I was careful enough. I had to be. Then I began finding money missing from my purse. He would take himself off to Norwich by train and go on a bender. I'd be rung up by the police or some pub and have to go and fetch him. He'd be terribly contrite afterwards, sort of maudlin, apologising abjectly for the bad time he was giving me."

"Didn't this rehabilitation centre help?"

"Yes and no. They only took a few National Health patients and there was always a waiting list. Sometimes, if I'd saved enough, I'd get him in there for a week, but it was a losing battle. He became more and more depressed. He would sit staring into space and I was at my wits' end to know what to do with him."

She paused, obviously distressed, and Rex said, "Don't go on now if you'd rather not." But she replied, "I'd like to get this bit over with.

"One night," she continued, "there was a ghastly gale blowing in from the north sea. It woke me up and I switched on the light. I turned to look at Dick in the next bed, but he wasn't there, I went all over the house calling his name and then I threw on a coat and went outside. The wind seemed to blow my voice away. We had a shed at the bottom of the garden and I found him lying there with an empty whisky bottle beside him. Heaven knows where he got it from. There was also an empty bottle of sleeping pills which our doctor had prescribed for me. Dick was still breathing, but he died in the ambulance on the way to hospital."

This time Rex said, firmly. "No more now, my love," and she answered, "But I still haven't told you what you wanted to know. About how I come to take on Chloe."

"Tomorrow," he answered. "Let's just leave it for now." He took her in his arms and, for a while, she slept.

12

SHE told Rex the rest of the story on their way home. In some ways it seemed easier. She felt more detached, as if she were imparting information to a listener who, although intensely interested and receptive, was not actually looking at her but at the road ahead, as he drove calmly and effortlessly back to London. The steady motion of the car — there were no sudden stops and starts with Rex — helped her to say what she had to say without too much hesitation or emotion.

"After Dick's death," she began, "I, like Steven, moved to London. It wasn't that I wanted to be near or dependent on my son. In any case, he was being sent all over the place. He simply kept a bed-sitter in Camden and I took the small flat I'm in now. I just felt that I'd had enough of the countryside. I wanted to see more people. I didn't want to lead a social life. I just wanted to feel life going on around me, to mingle with the crowd without being forced to meet the individual. I'm probably putting this awfully badly."

"You're not putting it badly at all. I understand completely."

"Well, after a while I thought I ought to do something a bit more positive. Get a job, although I was middle-aged and had no qualifications other than a smattering of nursing skills. At one stage, I thought of becoming one of those women who join an agency and get sent out as temporary 'carers', as I might have done when I had to give up St Thomas's. But then I realised it might land me back in the countryside again and I simply didn't want that to happen. I felt that being able to type wouldn't be a bad thing and so I went in for a crash course, but then I reckoned I had just about enough money to do a voluntary job and I managed to get one, at a citizens' advice bureau. It meant, of course, meeting a lot of individuals, but I tried not to become too involved. We were warned not to take their troubles home with us."

"What did you do with yourself in the evenings?"

"Nothing much. I got to know a few of the other residents in the house where I lived and, through them, occasionally one or two spare men asked me out to dinner or the theatre."

"Only one or two, Anna? I'm surprised they weren't all queuing up."

"There certainly wasn't any queuing. Besides, I wasn't interested in making any other relationships and they soon got the message. Steven was very good and came to see me whenever he could. He even persuaded me to make a trip to Paris later on, when he was sent there by his paper. Then, one day, towards the end of the '70s, he rang me early one morning. I could tell he was terribly excited and I thought it must be something to do with his job. But no, he was getting married. To a French girl, a model. Would I drop everything and come straight over for the wedding."

"So you did."

"Yes."

"Did you like her?"

"Rex, I hardly knew what to think of

her at the time. It was all so rushed. They were married at a French register office. Then there was a small reception at some friend's flat. Lysette, that was her name, didn't appear to have many relations. Certainly no parents, only a few rather sophisticated girlfriends, one who became Chloe's godmother. I really only saw enough of Lysette to know she was astonishingly beautiful and that Steven was head over heels in love with her."

"But she wasn't with him?"

"I . . . didn't think so. Oh, she gave all the appearance of a radiant bride, hanging on to his arm, all that kind of thing. I recall that she was dressed in a Dior outfit. Very smart, very clingy. She had a super figure."

"Not as good as her mother-in-law's, I bet."

"Nice of you. But remember, Rex, she was twenty-five years younger than I was. Afterwards, I couldn't help thinking that she wanted to marry Steven for the same reason that my mother wanted me to marry Dick."

"For the title?"

"Yes."

"Did you see much of them from then on?"

"No. They came to England sometimes, but my flat wasn't large enough to put them up so they stayed in hotels, which Lysette obviously found preferable. Occasionally, Steven came over to London alone for fleeting visits to see the editor of his English paper, but he always seemed anxious to get back to Lysette. He was doing quite well then, but I think he was never too sure of her, what she might get up to in his absence. He was intensely loyal, but from various things he sometimes let drop, I realised she must be extravagant, and when I visited them after Chloe was born it seemed to me that she had no maternal instinct whatsoever. She appeared annoyed that her so-called career had been interrupted, that she had missed chances through pregnancy. She was determined to get back to modelling and a series of young girls were engaged to look after the baby, usually *au pairs* in reverse: you know, starry-eyed English ones who were dying to get to Paris."

Anna paused for a while and then

continued, "One night, I shall never forget it. I'd gone to bed and the bell rang from the street. It was Steven. I let him in and waited for the lift to come up. He had Chloe with him. She was about three. She stood there, tired and bewildered, looking up at me with her enormous grey eyes. Then she put out her little arms and I gathered her up into mine."

"And that was that?"

"My commitment, my love for her, yes. We'd not seen enough of each other before to form a close bond. But that night I was sort of hooked. I felt such pity when I heard the whole story. But the love, in this case, came first."

"What had happened to the marriage?"

"Well, that night father and daughter were both so exhausted that I simply put Chloe to bed in the spare room and made up another for Steven on the couch in the sitting-room. In the morning he told me that he hadn't dared to leave Chloe in the care of their present *au pair*, who was unreliable, and that Lysette had run off with some theatrical producer, a much older man, who had promised to give her a leading part in his next production."

"A casting couch affair, if you'll forgive me putting it so baldly."

"Yes. But even if Lysette could leave Steven, I didn't see how she could have abandoned Chloe at that particular time, with no adequate person to look after her. But, as I said, she hadn't an ounce of maternal instinct in her, I'm afraid. Steven once admitted that when she was pregnant he had had a terrible time making her go through with it."

"Even though presumably she was Catholic and abortion would have been against her religion?"

"Yes."

"Has Chloe been with you ever since?"

"Oh, no. Lysette came back after a year or so. This part she was going to get never materialised. Well, I mean, how could it? She was a model, not an actress. Anyway, when this old roué let her down, Steven just took her on again. There had never been any question of divorce. I suppose that might have been more difficult than abortion but, in any case, Steven had probably reckoned the affair wouldn't last and was waiting to pick up the pieces. You see, he'd never stopped loving her. They tried again. She promised to turn over a new leaf. By that time Steven was back in London. He'd been promoted and had taken a flat in St John's Wood. Somehow, in all the interim period, he and I between us had coped with Chloe. At one stage he had suggested that I should move in with him, but something stopped me, thank goodness. Even though I thought it might have been nicer for the child to have all of us under the same roof, I felt Steven ought to have some life of his own. I used to have Chloe in the week and he took her on at weekends. Oddly enough, the child never questioned the arrangement. She seemed perfectly happy going from one of us to the other. Of course, she was still too young to understand what was going on, but I dare say she was aware how much we both loved her. I don't think she missed her mother at all."

"What happened when Lysette came back? Chloe couldn't have liked that very much, by the sound of it."

"Well, I think it was I who minded most. Children of that age do seem to accept change much more easily than grown-ups. I missed the little thing, although I still saw quite a bit of her. Our arrangement was sort of reversed and she came to me for weekends, whenever Steven and Lysette wanted to go away and the nanny they'd employed was off duty. But sometimes I felt as if I were living on a time bomb. I used to wonder how things were going in St John's Wood, but naturally I couldn't ask. I just sensed they weren't too good. I did my best to try to think of other things. That's when I started *Aftermath*. It was therapeutic. Stopped me worrying.

"Then, one day when Chloe was coming up seven, Steven came to see me one evening and said he wanted to take Lysette right away for a good long holiday. A friend of his had lent them a villa and a small boat on the Riviera and he felt it was just what Lysette needed. He didn't put it into so many words, but I guessed it was a kind of last ditch attempt on his part to save the marriage. Because, quite by chance, I'd happened to catch sight of Lysette one night dining with some other man when I was being taken out myself. I suppose it was silly of me but, even then, I didn't realise quite what a nymphomaniac she was. She did not, thank goodness, see me. Anyway, I expect she would never have imagined her mother-in-law to have been in the company of a member of the opposite sex, especially in such a sophisticated ambience. In any case, they only had eyes for each other.

"Steven asked me if I would come to St John's Wood just to be in residence while they were away. They had a much older nanny now who seldom wanted to go out and there would be nothing much for me to do. Not that I minded about that. I'd always been pleased to look after Chloe. 'Bring your writing,' I remember Steven saying."

"It seems to me, Anna," Rex broke in, "that you've been looking after other people most of your life."

"Perhaps. But it was always a pleasure to care for Chloe, that is, if it hadn't been for the *reason* behind it. Anyway, off her parents went. We had a few Postcards: blue skies, bare bodies and yellow beaches, which told us nothing.

You know, the X marks our bedroom window kind. It was late one night when I got a call from the French police. They were sorry to inform me that there had been an accident, a boating accident. Sir Steven Mallinder was in hospital, his wife missing at sea. It was one of those times when their nanny had actually gone out and I remember going and looking at Chloe asleep and fearing for her, for the future, for my son.

"I flew down to Nice," Anna went on. "Steven was distraught. The thing had got into the French papers and they were making much of it: *English baronet and his estranged wife*, as they said, although how they found out about that, I don't know. Then it sort of escalated. Suspicion fell on Steven. Apparently they usually had a skipper who went out with them, but on this particular day, for some reason or other, they went alone. So that counted against Steven for a start. There was an inquest where a whole lot of awkward questions were raised. Steven said that he had been having trouble with the boat's engine, that his wife had complained of a headache and had gone to the cabin to lie down. When he got the engine going again he went to find her and she wasn't there. The light was beginning to fade. He got on to the shore authorities by radio telephone and a sea and air search was made."

"Did they find Lysette?"

"No. Eventually a verdict of accidental death was brought in. I mean, there were no witnesses so I suppose it wasn't surprising. Steven came back to England but he was never the same. He tried to keep going for Chloe's sake. He became obsessed with her. All the love he'd had for Lysette was transferred to the child. But a year later he died. They said it was heart failure but to me it was more like heartbreak."

"Did Steven ever tell you more about the accident?"

She was silent for so long that Rex wished he had not asked the question. Then she said, quietly, "A little. Right at the end. He was very weak. I've never known exactly what happened and I've always kept it to myself."

"Because of Chloe?"

She blessed him for his sensitivity, his quick grasp of the burden she had carried ever since. "Yes," was all she answered, "because of Chloe."

13

THEY were late getting to Atherstone Lodge. Anna, having been only used to approaching the school from London, mistook a turning and Rex was obliged to make a detour. When they at last pulled into the gates, it seemed as though all the other pupils had been collected. Anna found Chloe sitting rather forlornly just inside the cloakroom entrance, her weekend and clarinet case beside her, while one of the younger mistresses hovered in the background. The child brightened on seeing Anna, who was full of apologies, explaining how they had driven straight up that day from Dorset.

As they walked out into the courtyard, Chloe said, "Is this friend of yours someone you once nursed with?" Then, seeing Rex standing by the car, she looked at Anna in bewilderment before blurting out, "You never said it was a *he*, Gran!"

Somehow, the introductions were not as easy as Anna had hoped. She could have kicked herself for not being more honest, for not giving Chloe more warning as to the identity of her companion. Rex courteously held out his hand and the child took it, but she did not smile. To her dismay, Anna saw an expression on her granddaughter's face which she had never seen before: a mixture of resentment, fear and even reproach.

On the way back to London, instead of maintaining her usual stream of chatter, Chloe simply answered, politely, the questions put to her: yes, she had had a good week; no, she had not played in any netball matches; yes, she would be playing her clarinet in the school concert at the end of term. But there was such an overall reserve in her manner that Anna was glad she had told Rex that they would not dine with him that night, but would lunch at the Hilton the following day. It was obvious that she had more than a little explaining to do and needed time alone with Chloe to give her a chance to rectify the unfortunate initial situation.

After Rex had been left at his hotel and Anna had taken over the wheel to drive them back to her flat, Chloe asked, "Who is he, Gran?"

"Someone I met in the war, darling. An American officer."

"Before you knew grandad?"

"No. When grandad was a prisoner of war."

"Why has he come to see you now?"

Why had Rex come, thought Anna. Why, indeed. It was for old times' sake, wasn't it? "He just thought it would be nice to . . . well, see each other again," she replied, somewhat lamely.

"Doesn't he have a wife?" Chloe's train of thought was palpably clear.

"No. I'm afraid she died."

"Does he want to marry you?"

Anna supposed the question was bound to come sometime, but she wished it could have been deferred a little longer. "He has . . . talked about it," she replied, guardedly.

"Will that mean you'll go and live in America?"

"Oh, Chloe, we haven't got as far as thinking about all that. At least, I haven't. I only saw Rex for the first time in fifty years last Monday. We've really just been exchanging news so far. Telling each other all that has happened to us since the war. But whatever our plans they would always include you."

"I don't like America," replied Chloe, firmly.

"But you've never been there."

"I know enough," came the enigmatic assertion, and then, as if a little further explanation was needed, the child added, "there's a girl at school whose grandfather lives in New York. She goes there sometimes and she says it's horrid. This old boy is always talking about money and wills and what will happen after he dies."

Anna gave a forced laugh. "But that's only one American, Chloe. They can't all be like that. In any case, Rex is different. When you get to know him you'll find out how nice he is."

But she could tell that her granddaughter was not convinced. On arrival at the flat, Chloe went straight to her bedroom where Anna could hear her rummaging about. There was no calling to each other over this and that, no friendly exchange of news or ideas. Anna busied herself in the kitchen, thankful that at least Maria had come up to expectations and done the shopping exactly according to the list she had left with her.

During supper Anna tried, as gently as possible, to steer the conversation in the way she wanted it to go, to explain how nice it was for people of her generation to reminisce. "We had a lot in common, Chloe," she said. "Rex knew Withyford. He knew your great-grandparents. While I was down there I went to look at my father's grave and I also saw a woman of about my own age whom I remembered very well as a girl."

"What else did you do?"

"We went further down the coast one day, into Devon. We saw a place where Rex had been stationed in the war, where there had been a tragedy when a lot of American soldiers were drowned practising for D-Day."

"D-Day?" Chloe frowned.

"Yes, back in June 1944. You'll probably learn all about it at school sometime. It was the day the British and American forces invaded France, the start of the campaign to liberate Europe, put paid to Hitler."

"Oh."

It was quite clear that Chloe was not in the slightest bit interested. Anna tried to be patient, to understand. It was history to the child. Old hat. After all, she reflected, she herself had never paid much attention to stories about the First World War when she had been growing up. It was only much later on that she became interested, when Cousin Hannah had told her that her mother had been in love with a married officer. It had been so surprising and had certainly answered a lot of Anna's speculations as to why Janet had married Robert Linsdale.

"Incidentally," Chloe said, suddenly, changing the subject, "Phoebe Bishop said if I wasn't doing anything tomorrow afternoon her elder sister would be taking her to a film and she wondered if I'd like to come too. It starts at one-thirty. The Plaza, Lower Regent Street."

Anna knew little about the Bishops, other than that they lived in Fulham. Phoebe had not been at Atherstone

Lodge long and was in a slightly higher form than Chloe. She was a plain, rather pert-looking girl with whom she did not feel her granddaughter would have had much in common. She could only suppose that because their respective homes were fairly near they had struck up some kind of friendship. She had no wish to prevent Chloe from going to the cinema with Phoebe Bishop and her sister, but it would interfere with their lunch with Rex.

"It wouldn't be possible to go to a later performance, would it?" she asked.

"Why?"

"It's just, well, Rex has asked us both to lunch with him at the Hilton."

"Can't you go alone? I'm sure the Bishops would have me to lunch if I explained the situation."

"Well, yes, I could," Anna replied, cautiously, "but I was rather hoping that you and Rex might get to know each other this weekend."

Chloe stared at her. "Rex is nothing to do with me, Gran. He's *your* boyfriend."

Jealousy was not an emotion which Chloe had ever shown before. Anna was both astonished and saddened. It seemed as if, just when at long last happiness might be within her reach, it was to be denied her. Then, suddenly, another emotion which she herself had rarely experienced, took hold. An uncontrollable anger welled up inside her. She thought of Rex's words: 'It seems you've been looking after other people most of your life'. She had always thought that at least caring for Chloe had never been a burden. Now, she was not so sure. The child was so antagonistic. She had assumed so much already about the relationship between her and Rex. That reference to *boyfriend*, for instance. It was both hurting and humiliating. What on earth would the child think if she had known that two nights ago her grandmother had actually slept with this stranger who had so unexpectedly come on the scene. But no, Chloe would surely never imagine that, even if she did know a great deal more about sex than Anna had at her age.

With an effort, she forced her mind back to the subject in hand. "If you think the Bishops will have you to lunch,"

Anna said, quietly, "I'll tell Rex."

"OK. I'll go and ring Phoebe now. I know it will be all right." Chloe jumped up with alacrity and left the table.

A little later on, Anna heard her playing the clarinet loudly in her bedroom.

14

"IT'S only natural," Rex said, as they started lunch. "I dare say Chloe felt bounced. I realise I shouldn't have arrived with you at Atherstone yesterday. It must have been a shock. She's had you to herself for so long."

"It's just as much my fault. And I know I oughtn't to have let her become so dependent on me. I should have arranged she saw more of her godfather, given her a wider social life."

"Anna, my love. Don't keep castigating yourself. Besides, surely her school is the answer to friends of her own age. It seems like an excellent establishment from all accounts. You've done or, rather, are doing such a splendid job. Apart from this present hiccup, Chloe looks all set to me to grow into a fine young woman. She might have had a difficult early childhood, but your care must have made up for so much, and she's obviously got her head screwed on."

"Oh, yes. She's intelligent all right, even though rather wayward and contrary at times." Anna toyed with some *hors d'oeuvre*.

"You needn't finish that if you don't want to." Rex pushed his own plate away and signalled to the waiter. "Anna," he went on, "I was hoping to have taken you both to a show tonight. In fact, I booked the tickets, but I've a feeling you'd like to spend another evening with Chloe alone. Maybe then you would both come out to lunch with me tomorrow."

She looked at him gratefully. He was behaving so well, trying to make things easier for her. It seemed terrible that after getting together again after all these years, after Rex had flown the Atlantic in order to do so, they had come up against this unexpected trouble.

Chloe appeared surprised that evening to find Anna by herself. As they sat down to supper, she asked, "What have you done with Rex?"

"He's gone to a show," Anna replied, carefully making no mention of the fact that they had both been asked to accompany him.

"Didn't you want to go?"

"Not particularly," she lied. Then, determined not to let the child interfere with their plans for Sunday, she added, "Rex is taking us both out to lunch tomorrow. I thought we might go to that new hotel in Epping Forest I've heard about. If it's fine, it should be a good place to walk afterwards."

Chloe said nothing. Never before, thought Anna, had a weekend seemed to drag by so awkwardly and slowly.

Fortunately, the lunch next day was not quite the disaster Anna had imagined it might be. By a happy chance, Rex started talking about the school in Lake Forest which his godson, Seymour McCutcheon junior, had once attended. Chloe actually asked a few questions, but on the way back to London she fell silent again. Although the Bishops had offered to take Chloe back with them to Atherstone that evening, Anna decided to drive the child herself and, leaving Rex at her flat, she was more than grateful for the welcome she received on her return. For all her independence, coming back to an empty home was something to which she had never grown quite accustomed.

They did not go out that night. Instead, she cooked Rex some scrambled eggs and, later on, it seemed the most natural thing in the world for him to make love to her again. Later still, he went back to the Hilton and, for the first time in many years, she knew she did not want to be left by herself any more.

She lay awake thinking. Her life had suddenly taken on a new dimension. It might be late, but surely it wasn't too late for this relationship which seemed, somehow, preordained. Chloe would have to accept the situation.

Difficult as she sometimes was, the child had never actually shown any signs of selfishness before. Moreover, Anna had promised her that she would always be a part of her plans. She meant that. But she knew that she and Rex would have to talk seriously about the future — and soon. So far, apart from a few vague suggestions, they had sidestepped the issue of how, when and where they would spend the rest of their lives. It was as if both were too overwhelmed by the miracle which had taken place, too scared of losing their sudden happiness, to discuss practicalities. This business of Chloe had brought them down to earth.

Rex, too, had evidently been thinking along the same lines for, when they walked in Hyde Park the next morning, he said, "Anna, when I flew here a week ago, naturally I didn't know what to expect. Although you were writing under your maiden name, for all I knew you might well have had a husband in tow. In fact, I'd have been surprised if you hadn't. If that was the case, I'd have just said hello and goodbye, although I would have hoped that there might have been a chance to talk about the past, about our last meeting. It seemed too good to be true to find that you were . . . well, fancy free."

"From the point of view of the opposite sex," she answered, guardedly.

Rex did not reply at once and then he said, "Chloe will surely get used to us. I've been wondering whether you might fly back with me to the States for a holiday, married or unmarried. I guess you'll always want to live in England and I'm prepared to do whatever you want.

I'm perfectly willing to arrange for the sale of my home in Lake Forest, although I'd love you to see it before it goes. How about both of us going back there for a holiday and then returning here. Marrying, say, at Christmas. That would give Chloe time to adjust, wouldn't it?"

On the face of it, she could think of nothing better, nothing she would sooner do. It had been such a long time since she had had a holiday. A real holiday. But there was more than one stumbling block and a particular one which she was well aware of and wouldn't go away.

"Rex," she turned towards him, an unaccustomed anger taking hold of her again, "I'd love to do that but . . . well, Chloe's half term is soon coming up."

"How long does she have?"

"A whole week. Well, ten days if you count two weekends."

"I suppose I could stay on," he said, "although I've never actually had a manager and if I'm to put the place up for sale it'll need a bit of organising. I'll also have to square things with Seymour about relinquishing my remaining commitment to the McCutcheon estate, although I don't foresee any problems there. I suppose we could take Chloe with us. If you're worried about the propriety angle, I mean grandmother possibly sharing accommodation with strange elderly man, how about marrying before going?" She could feel his urgency, his desire to get the issue settled. After all, they might not have that much time left. They were old, 'wrinklies', in fact, as Chloe might have said.

They had reached the Round Pond now. It was cold and blustery. Rain clouds scudded overhead. There were few children or grown-ups about and the scene which usually gave her such pleasure seemed oddly desolate. Could one ever recapture the past? Were they not both guilty of attempting the impossible? She had felt so very different at Withyford when it had just been herself and Rex. But somehow doubts had set in. Never before had the old adage, 'two's company, three's none', seemed so relevant. The impulsive side of her nature made her want to go to America with Rex now, this minute, almost as much as she had wanted him to make love to her in their youth. Then, with almost superhuman effort, she had suppressed her natural desires. Was she to deny them a second time? She certainly didn't want her granddaughter on this proposed trip. She wanted to be alone, free of responsibilities, with this man she had never forgotten and who, apparently, had never forgotten her.

Ways and means rushed through her mind, surprising her with their curious ruthlessness. To hell with her ridiculous conscience. It had been the bane of her life. She would look after Number One for a change. She would contact Chloe's godfather and guardian, Geoffrey Sheldon, an architect living near Oxford. He could do his duty for a few days, surely. And then, maybe, the Bishops would help out. The fact that Geoffrey was now divorced was a disadvantage, but he appeared to have a housekeeper who, on the few occasions Anna had met her, seemed to be quite a nice woman, if somewhat reserved. It would be a good opportunity for Chloe and Geoffrey to get to know each other better. She, Anna, should have initiated such a move long ago, prepared the child for the time when her grandmother would no longer be around. If Chloe started to be difficult about the arrangement, then that was just too bad. For once, Anna would be tough. Geoffrey was a responsible individual, she was sure. Her son would never have chosen an unsuitable godfather for his only daughter, would he? Although Anna could not help wishing that of the child's two godmothers, one had not been Chloe's own mother and the other a Frenchwoman called Martina Le Page, whom she had met at the wedding and not much cared for and who now, it would seem, had opted out of the whole situation.

"I'd love to come to America with you, Rex," she told him, as they started walking back to her flat. "I'll talk to Chloe about it next weekend. Perhaps it would be as well not to rush into marriage just yet, but I'm sure I could fix up for her to be taken care of while I'm away."

She could sense his relief. He took her hand and they walked on in silence. As they stood waiting to cross the

Kensington road, he held it even tighter, making her hold back where, ordinarily, she would have gone ahead. Having for so long looked after herself, to be cherished like this at her age seemed irresistible.

15

GEOFFREY SHELDON sounded wary on the telephone, even rather strange, Anna felt. I should have written, she said to herself. Not sprung a bombshell on him like this. I'm managing everything very badly.

When she explained that Chloe's half term was coming up and that she wanted to go to America, he repeated the word 'America' in a high-pitched disbelieving way, as if she might have been announcing she wanted to take off for Mars.

"With an old friend," she continued, doubtfully, and then, remembering Chloe's reproach, *You didn't say it was a he, Gran*, she went on quickly, "with an American officer who was stationed in England during the war."

There was a disconcerting silence on the other end of the line. Geoffrey, she realised, was a contemporary of Steven. He would have known nothing of the war. He was probably as uninterested in it as Chloe and would certainly never have imagined Anna in her youth or that she had ever had any relationship with a member of the opposite sex other than her husband. He must look on her as a complete has-been. She could almost hear him thinking: what is she on about at *her* age?

"I'm sorry," she heard him now saying, "but I'm afraid I can't have Chloe here at the moment. I've not been well."

This time it was her turn to say she was sorry. "I hope it's nothing serious."

"It's something which has been going on for some time," he replied, again in a guarded way. "In fact, I may shortly have to go into hospital."

Anna frowned. Why was he being so secretive? Was it cancer and he was scared of mentioning it? Some people, she knew, had a morbid fear of using the actual word, even went as far as to refer to it, euphemistically, as the Big C.

"I quite understand, Geoffrey," she said. "I do hope that you'll soon be well again. It was just a thought on my part, but I'm sure I shall be able to make other arrangements."

Other arrangements. *What* other arrangements, she wondered, as she put down the receiver. She could hardly foist Chloe on the Bishops for the whole of half term, even if they were prepared to have her. Besides, judging by the child's present reactions, she would be very upset and feel more than ever abandoned. Yet the thought of herself, Rex and Chloe all being together either in America or England made her quite certain that, however hard she tried, it wouldn't work — at least, not at the moment. Somehow, she had to reconcile her granddaughter to accepting, even liking, a completely new set-up. But how? Children were said to be resilient. But they were also obstinate, vulnerable and sometimes extremely hurting.

She wondered whether she might talk to Chloe's headmistress, Eve Wilson, about the problem. After all, she knew quite a bit about Chloe's background. She and Anna had had several long talks about it, both at Atherstone and in Anna's flat, where Eve occasionally came to dinner. But embarrassment held her back. Eve must be at least twenty years younger than she was. Though immensely sympathetic and broad-minded, it could be that she looked upon Anna rather as Chloe and Geoffrey Sheldon appeared to do. Some lines written by Lewis Carroll suddenly came into her head, the ones which ran, *You are old Father William . . .* She could easily substitute Granny Anna for Father William. She felt completely put in her place. Of course, her hair hadn't gone white yet and she certainly didn't keep standing on her head, but the question *Do you think at your age, it is right*? seemed somehow horribly apt.

That evening, when Rex took her to the theatre — she discovered that he had not, as she thought, gone alone to a show the previous Saturday but had managed to change the tickets — she tried to be lighthearted and conceal her fears. He was not, however, fooled. Back at her flat, she was obliged to tell him that she had failed to get any help from Geoffrey. For answer, he took her in his arms, saying, "Anna, *please*. Don't fret. You mustn't let Chloe come between us. Later on she would hate and blame herself for it. It'll be all right. I know it will. I'll stay on here until her half term. Then, why don't I go back to America and start the business of selling up and telling Seymour I'm going to live in England. That would give you and her more time alone for her to get used to the situation. After she's gone back to Atherstone, perhaps you could ask the Bishops to cope for a weekend or two and you could fly out to Chicago. We'll travel back here together and get married before Christmas."

His plans seemed so sensible, so practical and he was filled with so much enthusiasm for them that she allowed her fears to be assuaged. For the remaining time before he left she gave herself up to making the most of it. Her writing was firmly put to one side, and she indulged in a clothes-buying spree, a facial, a visit to a top hairdresser and she also saw to the updating of her passport. Yet, during the intervening weekend when Chloe was with her, she did her best to revert to the role of doting dependable grandmother, certainly not one who was having an affair.

Chloe, however, rather like Rex, was not to be fooled, especially as it was hard for anyone not to notice that Anna was looking both younger and prettier.

"You've had your side bits tinted," the child remarked, somewhat accusingly, when Anna collected her from school that Friday.

"Yes."

"Why?"

"I thought perhaps . . ."

The child broke in, "That Rex would like it."

To her chagrin, Anna found herself reddening. "A lot of women of my age have all their hair dyed regularly," she said, defensively.

"But I bet you wouldn't if your old boyfriend hadn't turned up."

"Oh, Chloe, please don't keep calling Rex my boyfriend. That's an expression for the young."

"But I said *old* boyfriend."

Anna slowed down, deciding not to overtake a lorry. If the child was trying to make her rattled, she was certainly succeeding in a most effective way. Anna supposed that she must have deluded herself all these years in thinking she was giving her granddaughter security. It seemed obvious that Chloe was extremely insecure. That was why she was hitting out. She, Anna, must be gentle, believe in Rex's assurance that all would come right. Supposing if she drew into the side of the road and took the child in her arms? Would that help? Perhaps not. It was probably important to avoid any melodrama. Time was what was needed. The trouble was that she was so conscious of its scarcity value. And sometime soon she would have to tell Chloe about her plans for going to Chicago without her.

The weekend passed. Rex called in once or twice but it was plain that his presence was unwanted, so far as Chloe was concerned. She was showing a side of her character which Anna had never suspected she possessed. Of course, she was Lysette's child just as much as Steven's. Anna realised that it was something she had been apt to forget. Was a certain hardness coming out in her now? As an all too devoted grandmother had she deluded herself into ignoring traits which were all too obvious to others? Chloe's next remark did nothing to dispel her new-found scepticism.

"Tell me," Chloe said on the way back to London, "if you and Rex were so keen on each other, why on earth didn't you marry him instead of my grandfather?"

It was a perfectly reasonable question, eminently logical. It was one which was bound to be posed sooner or later. Yet Anna found Chloe's clearsightedness disconcerting, even alarming. How did one reply to such a question? Sex had been a subject which had seldom cropped up between them. After all, Chloe was only ten. Yet Anna was now painfully aware that she hadn't been doing her duty in that direction, had somewhat shrunk from it, relying on the fact that girls of her granddaughter's age were so much more sophisticated than she had ever been. But exactly what sort of talk did go on, she wondered, in the dormitories at Atherstone. Before she had time to answer Chloe's question, Anna was soon to know.

"Do you actually sleep with Rex?"

As with the previous journey on Friday night, Anna slowed down. Playing for time, she enquired, "What makes you ask this?"

"Well, it's the sort of thing which happens, isn't it? But I didn't think it happened after . . . well, a certain age."

Summoning up all her courage and control, Anna replied, "It can happen at any age, Chloe, particularly when people love each other. I'm sorry we've never talked about it before. Have you discussed it with others?"

"Yes, of course. Phoebe Bishop knows all about it. Her sister told her. She does it with her boyfriend. I wouldn't like to catch you and Rex doing the same, though."

16

I *WOULDN'T like to catch you and Rex doing the same.* Chloe's words seemed to eat into her, printing themselves indelibly on her mind. Sometimes, during the past week before Rex's departure, she had felt like the Anna of the 1940s. Yet now, with him gone, she felt old, worn-out. His re-emergence into her life had jolted her, lifted her out of her habitual caution and reserve. He had somehow made *Aftermath* come alive in the most remarkable way. She couldn't help marvelling about the curious business of her writing the novel at all, its surprising success and then Rex happening to read it, which had brought him back to her.

But the difficulties with which she was now faced exercised her mind all and every day. With Chloe now home for half term, she was determined to do her best. Yet she felt confused: confused by the child's reactions to the situation, confused by her own. She worried about a certain ambivalence in her attitude, the doubting of a love for her granddaughter which she had hitherto taken for granted. How much of that might have been the result of natural compassion plus an over-developed conscience, which she had always put first? She recalled some lines — not this time by Lewis Carroll — which had been quoted in a book she had once read, the title and author long forgotten. Yet they had remained forever in her mind: *the dark sense of duty, greater than that of love*, the inference being that duty was black, all-prevailing and serious, while love was something free, light and wonderful — the two at odds with one another. She knew that she had invariably allowed the former to dominate the latter and was, in fact, still doing so.

Today, she could hear Chloe and Phoebe giggling together in the sitting-room as she prepared lunch in the kitchen, prior to taking them to a matinée. She wondered if Phoebe was regaling her granddaughter with further information about sex, whether Chloe was revealing her surmises about her grandmother's affair.

The unexpected letter which arrived next day upset Anna further. Postmarked Paris and written in perfect English, she read:

Dear Lady Mallinder,

I trust this will not be too much of a shock for you, coming as it does from Chloe's long lost godmother.

After the tragedy of Lysette's death and the mystery that surrounded it which was never satisfactorily resolved at the time, I was relieved to hear from friends that her daughter was being well taken care of by you and Steven. I realised that, living so far away, there was little I could do and I fear I allowed my responsibilities for the child's welfare, both moral and physical, to lapse. I must also confess — and here the writer broke into two words of French with a *Chère Madame* — that I doubted my ability to be of assistance, even after the death of your son. I sensed that you might well resent any interference from one who was so much closer to Lysette than to Steven.

You might also have thought she and I were both birds of a feather, used to the good life and neither of us maternal.

Forgive me if you think I am now acting on a whim.

Perhaps I am. But I am coming to London shortly and feel you would be interested in something I have to say. I should also like to see Chloe. She must be coming up eleven, no longer a baby. I am sure she is very pretty and will grow up to be a beauty like her mother. I have no child of my own but feel I could well make a rapport with a girl of her age. I discovered from international enquiries that you were still at the same address and would be delighted to hear from you.

Avec mes sentiments les meilleurs.
Martina Le Page.

A cold fear gripped Anna. What did she want to tell her? What business had this woman to see Chloe now, just when it seemed to suit her? All this reference to acting on a whim, having a rapport, saying that Lysette's death was never satisfactorily resolved. Did Martina Le Page have her own version of the boating tragedy? If so, what might she tell Chloe? The child remembered her father with love and respect, something which Anna had always been careful to foster, even if she had been unable to bring herself to encourage the same attitude towards Chloe's mother. They rarely spoke of Lysette, but now this virtual stranger who had turned up would probably want to change all that. But, whatever happened, Anna felt sure that Martina could scarcely be a good influence if she was still like the girl she had once seen at Lysette's and Steven's wedding. If memory served her rightly, Anna recalled she had been like the bride, with a model figure and, as only to be expected considering their mutual professions, astounding good looks, albeit marred by a coldness, even deviousness, in the light blue eyes. Yes, she and Lysette were certainly birds of a feather all right. Anna had been sorry to learn that Martina had been chosen as godmother when Chloe was born and had not been surprised that she had opted out of all commitment after Lysette's untimely death.

But was the woman, at this stage, making some kind of bid for possession or, at least, involvement with Chloe, simply because she had no child of her own, even though she had acknowledged that she was not maternal? Did she think she could step in and take over a ready-made offspring after someone else had ploughed through the long, often harrowing and exhausting years of bringing up a small being who was, Anna had to admit, scarcely any kind of intellectual companion — at least in the early stages. 'Gran', she remembered her granddaughter so often saying, 'tell it again', and Anna would sit patiently on the end of Chloe's bed, reiterating some story she had concocted which had made her, more than once, wonder whether it might not have been better to have embarked on writing a children's book, rather than a grown-up novel.

If only Chloe's godmother had been a sensible down-to-earth Englishwoman.

Then, Anna could have cheerfully gone off to America. But now she was not at all sure. In her emotional indeterminate state, wild visions of Chloe being abducted flitted through her mind. She checked them, but with effort. She ought to be thankful that when she had spoken to her about her plans the previous evening after Phoebe had gone home, the child had seemed to accept them, albeit with resignation. 'I thought that's what you'd be doing,' was all she had said.

When Rex made his customary call to her around nine p.m., Anna said nothing about Martina's letter. After all, what was there to say? She could not, would not, burden him with any more of her senseless worries. The re-emergence of Chloe's godmother would probably seem to him a splendid thing, someone else to share the responsibility, in fact most fortuitous, just at the moment. She gave herself up to listening to his voice, so eager and excited, as he kept reiterating how much he was looking forward to the following Wednesday when she was booked to fly out to Chicago and how glad he was that Chloe had accepted the idea.

But had she? Was she, Anna, deluding herself? During the rest of half term she did all she could to put up a front, wondering just how many other people she had known in life who had done the same. Her mother, for instance. What a sad existence Janet must have led. If only she could have married the army officer she had been in love with, she might have turned into a totally different character. And what about Steven, towards the end, fighting to keep some semblance of normality for the sake of his daughter, silent about what exactly had happened on that fateful last day of Lysette's life. Had they, as Anna suspected, had one hell of a row? Had his forbearance snapped? No, she would not think of that. Not now. The past was the past. It was the present which needed all her attention: when and how to answer Martina Le Page's letter.

Usually, Anna dealt with her correspondence at once but this letter needed thinking about. If only it had come a little later she would not have been at home. Martina Le Page was not to know that she was not there now. If she received no reply she would assume Anna was away and might even let the matter drop. The best thing to do was probably to go to the US as planned and write to the woman after her return. If Madame Le Page really wanted to see both her and Chloe then it would have to wait until a more convenient time. She certainly didn't want any meeting to take place now. A sixth sense told her that Martina probably enjoyed drama. There were always people who seemed to want to cause trouble and make life difficult for others, 'stirrers', as she remembered Steven once calling them.

Having decided on a course of action — or, rather, inaction — Anna still felt uneasy, however, as she left Chloe in the care of Maria while she went to the hairdressers on the last morning of half term; but it was nothing to the unease she felt as she returned and an excited Chloe greeted her at the door.

"Guess what, Gran. My French godmother telephoned. She wondered if you'd got her letter. She's coming round. I said you'd be back by eleven, that you were having your hair done because you were going to the States tomorrow. She asked who would be looking after me and I explained that I went to weekly boarding-school and I'd be staying with friends for two weekends. And then, you'll never believe this, but she said she was returning to France on Friday night and she would ask you if she could take me to Paris and put me on a plane back to London on Sunday evening. You know, I could travel as an unaccompanied minor or something."

17

"CHARMANTE," Madame Le Page said, "*parfaitement charmante*," after Anna had sent a reluctant Chloe into her bedroom to pack her case for school. "She is even prettier than I expected. She does you credit, *Madame*. You must be very proud of her."

Anna inclined her head slightly by way of acknowledgement, as she watched the Frenchwoman sitting opposite her, elegant and immaculate in a black and white check jacket and a pencil slim black skirt reaching to the knees of her beautiful legs, which she had somehow managed to display to maximum advantage to the viewer. Once a model, always a model, Anna thought. That was why Martina was only drinking orange squash. She had poured herself a strong gin and tonic.

Coming straight to the point Anna said, somewhat ungraciously, "Now that you have seen Chloe, *Madame*, what is it you wish to tell me? I gather it must concern her mother in some way?"

Martina Le Page sighed. "*Mais oui*," the deep curiously sexy voice replied. "*Pauvre* Lysette. She was my best friend. I fear she was *very* unhappy in her marriage to your son. When they went down to the *Villa Siga* that last summer, I was frightened for her. I don't quite know why, except that a little while before she had told me that Steven sometimes lost his temper with her."

Anna found herself springing to her son's defence. "Was that altogether surprising?"

"You mean, because of her . . . other affairs? You knew about them?"

"Steven was very loyal, but I had gathered she was unfaithful."

"But Steven had no ordinary temper, *Madame*. He was often violent. He hit her many times."

Anna frowned. "Did you come here to vilify my son?"

The cold blue eyes widened. "No, Lady Mallinder. I came because I am as sure as anyone could be that Lysette's death was no accident."

Anna remained silent as her unwelcome visitor went on, "You see, last September I happened to go down to St Tropez and, believe it or not, I was taken out with friends on the *Princess Hélène*, the same boat on which Lysette met her death. It had now been bought by the man who had once been its skipper, the self-same one who had *not* actually taken your son and daughter-in-law out on that fateful day. When I said, quite innocently, what a pity it was that he had been ill, he simply shrugged his shoulders, saying that Sir Steven had told him he wished to handle the boat himself. When I said I was surprised that this had not been reported at the inquest, he just shrugged his shoulders again, remarking that it was a long time ago and he had not wanted to get involved. He was not there when the accident happened and, so far as he was concerned, that was the end of it. I couldn't help feeling that there was more to his story and I brought it up again at the end of the day, when we were having a drink in a small bar. Actually Pierre Hervouët — that was his name — had more than one and he became, how do you say, a little loquacious, confidential? He and I were somewhat apart from the others and he admitted that he hadn't wanted to get involved because Sir Steven was a very jealous man. I suppose I am outspoken, but I couldn't help asking, 'Of you?'. He shrugged once more. I knew at once what he was inferring. Naturally, he wanted to keep out of any proceedings, especially as he had a wife of his own at that time.

Anna took a long pull at her drink.

"I realise, Lady Mallinder," Martina went on, "that Lysette was somewhat of a nymphomaniac, but she could not help her nature. She may have had many faults, but not enough to be *murdered* for them."

Anna tried to make her voice sound normal. She was quite surprised to find herself speaking at all, as she asked, "Why have you come to tell me this?"

Martina's eyes avoided hers. She looked out of the window. "I felt I owed it to Lysette. I did not see why you, as Steven's mother, should remain unaware of what really happened. I knew he had died but I also felt, perhaps belatedly, that I should try to find out how Chloe was faring. As I mentioned in my letter, I am not maternal, but I believe I could now be of assistance. I am of a younger generation and could introduce Chloe into the French way of life."

Younger generation, indeed. What was the woman getting at? That she, Anna, was too old to be in charge? Perhaps she was, but she was as sure as she was of anything that Martina Le Page was unsuitable to have the care of any child. She was too much a woman of the world, rich — or appeared to be — self-confident, sophisticated and was, or had been, married, for she wore a wedding ring, although there was no mention of any husband.

Anna stood up. "Now that you have told me why you have come, *Madame*, I must ask you to leave."

Martina also rose, but slowly, her beautiful body somehow becoming upright effortlessly, poised, as it were, to make a graceful exit.

"Forgive me, *Madame*," she remarked, as she turned towards the door, "I fear

I have upset you. No doubt my spur-of-the-moment idea of giving Chloe a weekend in Paris does not meet with your approval."

"No," Anna answered, "it does not."

"Never mind. As the child gets older, I am sure her mother's native country will have even more to offer her."

At that moment, while Anna was thinking: not over my dead body, Chloe herself appeared, expectantly, from her bedroom.

"*Au revoir, chèrie*," Martina said. "I think perhaps your *grandmère* would prefer you not to visit me just yet."

The child looked hurt, nonplussed. After Martina had gone, she asked, accusingly, "Why Gran? I know Miss Wilson is all for us widening our experience. It wouldn't be as if I'd miss any school. And I'm sure the Bishops would understand. I think it was mean of you to say I couldn't go."

"I'm sorry, my dear." Anna turned and walked into her bedroom, closed the door and lay down. If she cancelled her trip to America at this short notice, what explanations would she give to Chloe, the Bishops and Eve Wilson, to whom she had written with precise details of her itinerary? But above all, Rex? Was she to let him down a second time — and again in mysterious inexplicable circumstances? Should she not stifle her fears? There was no reason to think Madame Le Page was any real threat. At least, not at the moment. She surely wouldn't want to abduct Chloe. The worse she could do might be, later on, to tell the child just what she had told Anna about Steven and Lysette. At the moment, she was simply a mischief-maker. That was all. Perhaps the best thing to do would be to have a word with Eve Wilson when she drove Chloe back to Atherstone. It needn't take long and it wasn't as if it was the beginning of term, when Eve might not have time to see her. She would be as brief as possible, just ask Eve to keep a special eye on Chloe while she was away. Anna picked up the telephone and managed to make an appointment through the school secretary.

As she had feared, however, her granddaughter put up more than a little resistance to starting back to school an hour earlier than usual. "But why, Gran? You said you'd written to Miss Wilson about all your arrangements."

"Yes, but I just want to confirm one or two things. Please, Chloe, don't make difficulties."

"I still don't see why you couldn't have let my godmother take care of things now she's turned up. She's ever so nice. I'm sure she didn't like the way you refused her offer."

Almost, Anna's nerves snapped. "Chloe, please," she said again. "Have you got everything ready? I want to leave here by five."

All through the day Anna changed her mind about her forthcoming trip from hour to hour. It wasn't until she was in Eve Wilson's study that the decision was made. Anna found herself saying more than she intended, yet the relief of being able to unburden herself to this extraordinarily understanding woman made it impossible to hold back. She told Eve about Rex, about Chloe's reaction to their affair, about Geoffrey Sheldon's illness, about Martina's visit and about her own belief, albeit based on nothing save intuition, that the woman was up to no good and would be a bad influence on any growing child. Only over Martina's allegations concerning Steven did Anna become less informative, doing her best to brush them aside. Yet, afterwards, she realised that Eve might well have formed her own ideas about that.

"You won't be happy if you go tomorrow, will you?" she said.

"No."

"Then why don't you just postpone things, not cancel them. You can simply tell the Bishops that your plans have been altered and you'll be going to America later on. I shouldn't think that will bother Chloe. Besides, I've always found that once kids are back at school, they usually tend to forget many of the home problems that might have cropped up. Then you can go and see your solicitor, ask his advice about guardianship or wards of court. I don't quite know how long that takes, but I imagine it often has to be pushed through quickly."

"I'd thought of that, but it seems so melodramatic. I could be making a mountain out of a molehill."

"I wouldn't have thought anything was melodramatic if it gives you peace of mind."

"I suppose not."

"And Anna, if you like, I'd be prepared to step in as a kind of deputy since you've said that Geoffrey Sheldon's ill. I'm interested in Chloe. I know she might be a bit of a handful and difficult just now. But children who have a lot in them often are. It isn't really quite the thing for a headmistress to become personally involved with any one pupil but, in this case, I'd make an exception. I give you my word that I'd do my best."

18

"BUT why, Anna? What's happened, my love? You're not ill, are you?" There was fear, disappointment and disbelief in Rex's voice. "Is it Chloe?" he went on. "I thought she'd accepted your coming here." Anna hoped she was wrong, but she thought she sensed a tinge of exasperation in his last question.

"No. I mean yes. Chloe has accepted my trip. I'm postponing it due to completely unforeseen circumstances. I'll do my utmost to fly out in a week or so's time."

"Have you actually altered your ticket?"

"I'll attend to that first thing in the morning. This has only just cropped up. I want to make certain about extra arrangements for Chloe in my absence. Possibly settle for another guardian or even make her a ward of court."

"What?"

"A ward of court. I just don't know at the moment. I shall try to see my solicitor tomorrow. Her French godmother has suddenly come on the scene after all these years and seems bent on making trouble."

"What kind of trouble?"

"I'm not sure, Rex." She wondered if perhaps he was thinking her an hysteric, whether, in fact, she was. "It's to do with the past, darling," she went on, uncertainly. "I can't explain on the telephone, but once this woman's gone back to France, I'll feel happier."

"When will that be?"

"I understand Martina Le Page — that's her name — is leaving on Friday. She wanted to take Chloe with her for the weekend."

"And bring her back?"

"No. Send her alone, as an unaccompanied minor, or so she said."

"Where is this woman staying?"

His quick thinking, reasoning and sagacity confounded her. How would she know if Martina had returned to France? Why, she didn't even know where she was staying. What a fool she had been not to ask.

"I'll find out," she replied, lamely.

But how, she thought. Would it mean telephoning every hotel in the West End?

Suddenly Rex, as if regretting his initially laconic cross-questioning, was all solicitude. "Anna, I think I'd better come back now. You seem to be having problems."

"No!" She was surprised at her vehemence, as she almost shouted, "I can handle it."

And even if I can't, she kept saying to herself as she eventually put down the 'phone, this is something I have to try to deal with alone, before I can go forward into any future, however short or long that might be. I had a son who grew up under difficult circumstances. Probably, because of them, he was never as balanced as I thought. I have pledged myself to take care of his daughter. I can't run out. Not now, however much a new seemingly halcyon way of life beckons. The young, surely, should have priority. The old may have made a mess of their lives, but whatever they have done, whatever disappointments they have suffered and whatever personal failings they might have, that's no excuse for abandoning the younger generation. Besides, you'd never feel happy if you did — and you love Chloe, don't you?

The next morning Anna telephoned Nicholas Clarke, her solicitor, and also the travel agency through whom she had booked her trip, finding that she had more success with the former in that Nicholas agreed to see her at 2 p.m. The business of negotiating a refund for her ticket seemed a minor problem compared to the urgency of talking to her solicitor.

She found him, affable and courteous as ever, as he stood up when she entered his office and held out a hand.

"How nice to see you, Anna, although I gather you've come about something urgent."

"Well, yes, Nicholas. I want to go out of the country for a while and I'm concerned about Chloe's welfare in my absence."

He did not seem unduly surprised. "Because of Geoffrey Sheldon's illness, I imagine," he remarked, as they sat down.

"Geoffrey Sheldon?" She was nonplussed. "How did you know he was ill?"

"Because he wrote to me. As a matter of fact, I was just about to write to you. He said you had asked him if he would have Chloe to stay while you went to America."

"Yes, but I realised he couldn't. He told me he might have to go into hospital. He didn't exactly say what was wrong."

"He didn't like to, Anna. That is why he got in touch with me. He wishes to renounce his guardianship of Chloe. He wants me to tell you how sorry he is that he is unable to fulfil any more obligations towards her."

"But why?"

"Because he has Aids."

"Oh, my God."

"I imagined that was why you wanted to see me, that perhaps he had changed his mind about not feeling able to tell you himself."

"No." She was silent, shattered. It was as if, at this particular moment in her life, strange forces were getting together to conspire against her. Once again, uncharacteristic emotions vied with each other to make her confused. I've done my best, she thought. What a pity I couldn't have been more selfish, more hedonistic all those many years ago, let Rex make love to me. What the hell if I'd had a baby. It might not have been the end of the world, especially as I've learned he wasn't married and would always have stood by me. My father liked him and he was a good judge of character. Now it seems as if I'm all set to deny a second chance of happiness.

A second chance. She remembered seeing the words on a poster in the public library just after *Aftermath* was published. It advertised courses for women of a certain age who might want to go in for a spot of further education, who might try for an O or an A level. She did not think she would have been brave enough to embark on them and had been grateful that it would appear, in writing a novel which was showing every sign of success, a whole new career seemed to be opening up for her when she was getting on for seventy.

Suddenly she became aware of letting her mind wander, of Nicholas looking at her, expectantly.

"Anna," he said, "what makes you

particularly worried about Chloe at this moment?"

"Yesterday her French godmother turned up out of the blue."

"And so?" He drew her out, quietly, patiently.

"She . . . wanted to take Chloe to Paris for a weekend, after all these years of silence."

"And you refused?"

"Of course."

"Did she give any reason for turning up at this point?"

Anna hesitated. She wasn't going to tell Nicholas anything concerning Martina's revelations about the accident. How could she say that something horrific which she had suspected or, rather, tried not to suspect, had now, according to this wretched Frenchwoman, been practically confirmed, that she felt that Martina had it in her power to destroy the image of Steven which she had been so careful to build up for his daughter's sake. The word blackmail, hideous and frightening, rose in her mind.

"I think she is a mischief-maker," Anna replied, at length, aware that Nicholas was watching her carefully. "She did not strike me as being at all a suitable person to care for a growing child."

"Why do you think she wants to now?"

Anna could feel the tell-tale flush coming to her cheeks, knew that Nicholas sensed that she had not come out with the whole story, probably had his own versions of the mystery surrounding Lysette's death. "I'm not exactly sure," was all she replied. "I simply feel she's a dangerous woman. I'm concerned that Chloe should have further protection."

"Besides a new guardian?"

"I had thought about a ward of court."

"Suppose," he answered, "we appoint a new guardian first. Had you anyone in mind?"

She looked at him, miserably. "Would it be too much . . . ?" she faltered.

"Of course not, Anna. I'll be only too pleased to try and help over Chloe although, I wonder, do you know of a woman who might be able to back me up? Share the responsibility?"

Quietly, she replied. "Chloe's head-mistress, Eve Wilson, is very supportive."

19

NEVER before had Anna felt glad to have woken up with a heavy cold or, possibly, 'flu. Her head ached and her throat was sore. It seemed a splendid explanation to give to everyone for having cancelled her flight, while still allowing Chloe to spend the weekend with the Bishops, as arranged. She could truthfully tell Rex that it was a mercy she hadn't travelled. It also gave her time to see whether she could do any checking-up on the seemingly malevolent Martina.

Yet Anna realised she had so little to go on. Nicholas Clarke had taken her worries seriously and was prepared to become Chloe's new guardian; but she was still unsure whether, in her heightened emotional state, he privately thought she was tending towards the theatrical. He had not, for instance, considered it necessary, at this stage, to make Chloe a ward of court. On the other hand, he had not been present at yesterday's extraordinary meeting. Should she have told Nicholas more, repeated what the wretched woman had said, all that she herself had always suspected? Might it not have been better, certainly fairer? After all, Steven was dead. The inquest on his wife could hardly be reopened. Nothing could harm him now. But Martina Le Page had it in her power to harm Chloe — and Chloe must be protected at all costs.

Chloe! It seemed that everything always came back to Lysette's and Steven's daughter. Was it possible, Anna thought and not for the first time, that in putting all her love and energy into bringing up her orphaned grandchild she had become blind to the girl's faults? Did Chloe's recent behaviour mean she was hopelessly spoilt — all the spoiling done by her grandmother? Moreover, had Anna refused to accept that it was possible the child had far more of her mother's make-up in her than her father's. Certainly, in looks, Anna was beginning to see a striking resemblance to Lysette: those enormous eyes, the mannerisms, particularly the one where she spread out her hands in a gesture of explanation. That was decidedly French, wasn't it?

While Anna was turning all these things over in her mind, the telephone rang beside her bed. She stretched out an arm and picked up the receiver.

"Hullo?"

The line went dead.

Anna knew it was the sort of annoying thing which occasionally happened, but she could not help wondering whether it could possibly have been Martina checking up on *her*, rather than the other way round. Did the woman want to find out whether Anna had actually left for America? Yet why? What motive could she have? Did she really expect money for keeping silent over Steven? She hardly looked as if she was short of a few francs, but one could never tell. Appearances were so often deceptive. In the highly unlikely event of Anna allowing Chloe to go to France this weekend, would Martina then have said, point blank, that she would keep her recent discoveries to herself — for a certain sum? During the brief time she had spent in Anna's flat, she must have quickly sized up the situation: that Anna was defensive and anxious to protect her grandchild, come what may. Just supposing it *had* been Martina on the telephone a few minutes ago finding that Anna had not gone to America after all. Would it have made the woman feel she had the upper hand, that her victim would hardly go to a solicitor and confess that she feared her son was — or might well have been — a murderer?

Feeling more and more wretched both mentally and physically, Anna staggered along to her kitchen, made herself a cup of tea and took it back to bed with her. She remembered that Chloe had said she had told Martina that it had been arranged she should stay with friends at the weekends while Anna was away. Had the child given her godmother the Bishops' name?

When Anna rang them to explain that she had postponed her trip but would be most grateful if they could still have Chloe on Friday as she was down with 'flu — it seemed best to opt for the more serious complaint — she felt she could hardly go into her fears about her granddaughter's French godmother. Mrs Bishop was such a no-nonsense down-to-earth woman. Even if no one else did, she might well consider Phoebe's friend's grandmother somewhat eccentric, certainly impulsive or maybe even mutton dressed as lamb, since she had met Anna once or twice lately looking rather more fashionable than usual. Mrs Bishop would be sure to know the reason why Anna wanted to go to America. Chloe would have told Phoebe and Phoebe would have told her sister and her mother. And her mother would have thought: old ladies coming up seventy did not — or should not — go chasing after old boyfriends of seventy plus. Mrs Bishop would have felt sorry for Chloe and wished to step into the breach for that reason, but she would not have felt sorry for Anna. Mrs Bishop was something of a do-gooder. Time was when Anna considered she herself was a little inclined that way. But not now. Perhaps, after all these years, the real Anna was coming out.

That night the customary telephone call from Rex was not the happy carefree one of a few days ago. He sounded distant, both in miles and manner. Afterwards, she panicked a little. Had their reunion simply been a brief interlude? Could they now ever recapture the sheer delight and pleasure of being in each other's company again? And it was her fault, wasn't it? Rex's past, sad as it might have been, was behind him. Hers was still very much with her: the mystery surrounding the death of her daughter-in-law, the question mark over her son and, above all, the tangible ever-present result of their union and the necessity for looking after her.

Suddenly, Anna's mind turned to Geoffrey Sheldon and his surprising unfortunate illness. She ought, perhaps, to go and see him or, at least, write. She had always imagined that Steven would have chosen a godfather for Chloe with an impeccable reputation. Now, she wasn't so sure. The uncertain feeling of not being sure of anything took hold of her once again. She knew she had no right to judge the man. People were as they were, but had Steven really known Geoffrey? And had she ever really known her own son? After he had gone out into the world and married so impulsively, there had seemed no time for any serious discussions other than those about Chloe. Even towards the end, they had only spoken of the child.

Anna recalled Steven's last words, as she had sat beside his bed the night before he died. He was far from coherent. The drugs they had given him had made it difficult to understand what he was saying. Yet one word kept coming through the jumble of others. It was 'sorry'. Had he been saying he was sorry for leaving Anna to cope? Or was he saying he was sorry about the accident? For it was obviously on his mind. Then, suddenly, he had struggled to sit up, had looked straight at her and said, this time quite clearly, 'Chloe must never know'.

Throughout the years Anna had tried to kid herself that what he had meant was that Chloe must never know about her mother's affairs. But reason told her he probably meant something far worse, that whatever had happened on the *Princess Hélène* on that final day had not been a straightforward accident. Now, after

Martina Le Page's disclosures, it seemed to Anna that it was more than likely that Steven had attacked his wife because of her infidelity. He might not have meant to kill her. The thing had got out of hand. He had simply reached the limit of his endurance. He had taken Lysette away to try to save their marriage, only to find that she was carrying on with the skipper of the boat on which they were meant to be enjoying a second honeymoon.

The morning wore on. Anna managed to telephone the Bishops and found, rather to her surprise and mortification, that Phoebe's mother was understanding and sympathetic. Anna also left a message with Eve Wilson's secretary, but felt too wretched and listless to try to find out anything more about Martina Le Page.

When evening came, she took out the thermometer which was usually only used for Chloe and found that she had a far higher temperature than she expected. She dozed on and off fitfully, waiting for Rex's call.

But the call did not come. Nine, ten,

eleven and midnight passed while she fretted, half asleep, half awake. “You’ve messed it up,” she said to herself in the early hours of the morning, “messed everything up completely.”

20

"I'M sending in a nurse," Dr Fenton said.

"Nurse?" Anna replied in a whisper.

"Yes. I don't want you left alone. You have virus pneumonia."

"But I . . . "

Alan Fenton held up his hand. "No 'buts', Anna. Leave it to me. I'll ask your daily help to stay until someone arrives. I'm going to give you an injection and leave you with a few pills and a prescription for some more. Take two now and another two in a couple of hours."

She winced. The stabbing pain in her left side was acute. All at once, it seemed easier to give in rather than argue. She heard him talking to Maria in the hall before letting himself out. When the girl started to come into her bedroom she told her to keep away. "Maybe infectious," she said, whispering again.

Whatever her distress, it was second nature to Anna to consider others first.

She swallowed two pills with the aid of a glass of water by her bed and then lay back on the pillows. It was a long time since she had been ill. In fact, she couldn't remember being laid quite so low, except in the war when she had been sent to a nursing-home, and even that had not been for a physical illness. Over the years she had come to the conclusion that she was basically fairly tough. Her unhappy marriage and difficult widowhood had taught her, somehow, to cope. She had not gone under, although there had been many times when she had felt it would have been easy to do so. Now, with Rex seemingly out of communication again, feeling weak and giddy every time she tried to stand up, the desire to give in was overwhelming.

When, in her semi-conscious state, she heard the bell from the street ring, she vaguely imagined it was Dr Fenton's nurse. She had lost count of time. She heard Maria answer it, press the buzzer to permit entry and then the whine of the lift starting up almost immediately. She became aware of the front door of the flat opening and a man's voice. Could Dr Fenton possibly have sent a *male* nurse?

The next minute Rex was standing at her bedroom door.

"You are not safe, Anna," he said, as he sat down on her bed and took her hand, "to be left alone."

She closed her eyes. For quite a while neither of them said anything more. She gave herself up to the sheer relief and luxury of having him there to take care of her and the situation.

Rex organised everything. He rang Dr Fenton, explained his presence, cancelled the nurse, moved into Chloe's room, gave Maria money and a shopping list and, within forty-eight hours, had Anna sitting up in bed, weak but no longer despondent.

"But what about your commitments back home?" she asked him that evening.

"All taken care of," he replied, cheerfully. "In fact, if it hadn't been for wanting you to come over for a holiday and see the place before it went, I knew it was now perfectly all right for me to leave it in the agent's hands. Everything can be concluded by remote control."

Presently, he continued, "Anna, suppose you tell me all that happened here since I left. I gather the godmother's visit was pretty disturbing."

"Yes."

"I suppose she didn't really want to take Chloe back to France with her, did she? I imagine she wanted to get at you somehow."

"Yes."

"About what happened to Lysette?"

"How did you guess?"

"Dearest Anna, it wasn't very difficult. I realised you'd never told me the whole story or, at least, your version of it. Perhaps now you might feel able to?"

She told him then, everything: her fear at the time of the tragedy, her increasing suspicion ever since, Steven's last words, Martina's revelations, the importance of keeping it all from Chloe.

He was silent for a while. He seemed to be thinking, hard. "Anna," he said, at length, "I'm not sure how much a child should be shielded. Oh, don't get me wrong. Naturally you want to keep all these conjectures from Chloe, especially now, and you certainly don't want her learning of any from the wrong person. Incidentally, you've no proof, have you, that this Martina woman hasn't fabricated her story, although it would seem to tie in with much of what you've always suspected. But having brought Chloe up to idolise her father, it could be very distressing for her to learn later on that he was no saint — even though possibly he might have been guilty of a *crime passionel.*"

"Yes. I realise that."

"You see, I was thinking of a friend of mine back in the States. All his life he'd been taught that his father was a super guy. Then, when he was coming up seventy, he received a letter from some woman informing him that his half-brother was dead. He replied saying he didn't have a half-brother. Back came another letter from the daughter of this chap enclosing evidence in the form of an agreement drawn up some eighty years previously concerning some affair my friend's father must have had in his youth. I can tell you, it just about threw him. He was never the same. He was a widower by then and living alone. He died an unhappy, disillusioned man. If only someone could have told him earlier on about human nature, human frailty, that these things sometimes happened more often than many people realised, it would have been so much better. It was the fact that it was all hushed up, kept from him, that made him feel hoodwinked."

"I see. But you've already said that Chloe mustn't know anything now."

"No. Of course not. But I don't think you should let this French godmother intimidate you. She's probably only a mischief-maker, trying something on, getting you to rise to the bait. There are certain characters like that. Incidentally, while you've been recovering, I discovered she was staying in some small hotel off the Cromwell Road, from which she and a man checked out en route for Heathrow the day after she called on you."

"But Rex, how on earth . . . ?"

He cut her short. "I told you, Anna, I wasn't an intelligence office on Ike's staff for nothing. I got on to one of your detective agencies. They were good. Let's hope you won't hear any more from Martina but, if you do and she becomes a nuisance, then you simply hand it all over to your solicitor who's agreed to become Chloe's guardian. I think you should try to get it across to the child that Martina Le Page would not appear to have her best interests at heart and should she ever try to contact her direct, then she must let you know immediately."

"Wouldn't that make Chloe liable to do just the opposite?"

"Not if it's handled right. Look, Anna, if you like, I'll have a word with Chloe. Do please remember, my love, that you are no longer alone."

I am no longer alone. I am no longer alone. She hugged the words to herself after Rex had gone out to do some slightly more sophisticated shopping than Maria. When the telephone rang, she was able to answer Eve Wilson's enquiry after her health quite cheerfully. "I've been a bit rough, Eve, but I'm much better now. Rex has returned from the U.S. I really don't deserve the splendid way I'm being looked after."

"I think you probably do, my dear, and I'm glad. And I want to say that I think you'll find Chloe much more amenable when you next see her. She and I have had a long talk. The poor child was terrified she was going to lose her only security: you. That was why she was so thrilled to have this somewhat dubious godmother turn up. When I explained how nice it would be for her security to be re-inforced by a step-grandfather, I could see her beginning to look on the situation in a different light. She's never had anything personally against your Rex. In fact, she admitted at the end of our talk that he was 'sort of nice'. When I said she was really jolly lucky, do you know what she replied?"

"No."

"She said, 'I suppose I am. Gran certainly is'."

Anna put down the receiver at the end of their conversation. 'Sort of nice', even though a fairly cautious commendation, somehow seemed entirely right and much more than she could possibly have hoped for.

21

THE house near Richmond Park was not large, but light and airy so that it gave the impression of spaciousness. There was also an attractive garden running down to a small stream at the bottom. Anna, having been accustomed for many years to living in much more confined conditions, was at first slightly overwhelmed at the thought of looking after such a place, when she and Rex were shown over it by the estate agent. It was a long time since she had coped with an establishment of this size, but Rex's enthusiasm for Charlton Lodge soon dispelled her reservations. More and more, she was coming to appreciate that his positive attitude to everything seemed to carry him along, as well as all with whom he came into contact. Difficulties were regarded simply as 'life'. Problems were always minimised. Advantages explored. Moreover, they both realised that there was already one enormous advantage in taking the house: its easy accessibility to Atherstone Lodge. It was unthinkable that there should be any alteration to Chloe's schooling.

Having put in a bid for their potential new home, they took her to see it on a second inspection. Anna was surprised by her enthusiasm, until the real reason emerged. "Did you notice, Gran," she said, "that there are some riding stables round the corner?"

"No. But you never told me you wanted to ride, my dear."

Chloe flushed. "Well, I thought it would all be too complicated living in London, besides too expensive."

It seemed like the old Chloe coming back, Anna felt, the more thoughtful and appealing child she had known.

The three of them spent the weekend at an extremely comfortable nearby hotel. Rex arranged that they should now do this every time Chloe came home, partly because it solved the problems of sleeping quarters in Anna's flat, and partly because he was concerned that she should be relieved of as many domestic chores as possible since her illness.

As soon as they knew that their offer for Charlton Lodge was accepted, Rex reserved accommodation at the same hotel on a more permanent basis, as it seemed a good arrangement whereby Anna could put her flat on the market and they would be on the spot to organise the move.

Euphoria took hold of Anna once again. She chose yellow wallpaper and pale green silk curtains for the sitting-room and saw to the installation of built-in bookcases and a desk in Chloe's room, as well as making plans for the garden, while an amused and delighted Rex seemed ready to indulge her every whim.

"They're like a couple of love-birds," Chloe confided to Phoebe Bishop one evening when they were in their dormitory at Atherstone. "It makes one a bit sick sometimes, but it'll be nice living at Charlton Lodge. You'll have to come and stay. I'm going to learn riding after Christmas. Gran seems a lot more willing to let me do things. I think Rex must be rolling. He's always saying, 'Go ahead, darling', if Gran thinks she's being a bit extravagant. Of course, I suppose having sold his big place in the States means he can afford to splash out."

"That's nice. Have you seen any more of that funny godmother who turned up?" enquired Phoebe.

Chloe frowned. "No. I don't quite know why Gran took against her so much, but I suppose she was a bit over the top. She was very glam, but I don't really mind about not being allowed to go to France, not now, not when I can learn to ride."

"When's the wedding?"

"The Saturday after next. In a register office. There'll only be me and Miss Wilson and Gran's solicitor who's been made my new guardian, although I can't see I need another one now, since Rex has come on the scene. Then the happy pair are going off on the Monday to Withyford for a few days."

"Will they share the same bedroom now, do you suppose?"

"Of course. Although I think they do already, that is, when I'm not around."

Phoebe rolled over on her bed. "My

sister thinks it's all a *hoot*."

The objects of the 'hoot' were, at that moment, looking at pictures in a Bond Street art gallery. At first, Rex had considered shipping some of his own across the Atlantic, but had thought better of it and arranged to have them put up for sale. "I don't want reminders," he said to Anna. "My house in Lake Forest was fine in its way, but I've come to realise it wasn't a home. Charlton Lodge is, or will be, thanks to you. And when we're settled in you'll take up your writing again, won't you?"

She smiled. "I don't know. Maybe I'll have enough to do. Or maybe I'll just be too happy."

"Anna, you must. I shall goad you into it. Lock you into that little room in the attic which would make a splendid study."

"But what about you? I thought that might be your hideaway."

"I don't think I want one. I'm not creative like you. I can always use that small alcove off the sitting-room for whatever paperwork I do. Besides, it mightn't be much unless . . . " he hesitated, a little embarrased, "I decide to dig into the Slapton Sands affair a bit more, go to your Imperial War Museum and look up whatever records they have."

"And then write about it?"

"Anna, it would only be a factual account from someone who was actually there at the time. As I said, I'm no scribe, but it's occurred to me that there must be an awful lot that went on in the last war which people never got to hear about. On the other hand, I might become a complete man of leisure and play golf. It's a pity I'm a bit too old to take up riding again and go out with Chloe."

If it had not been for the public place they were in, she felt she might have kissed him.

Their wedding took place in an atmosphere of great harmony and goodwill the weekend before Chloe broke up for the Christmas holidays. Anna wore beige with a large beige felt hat decorated with russet-coloured ribbon. Chloe, who had been allowed to choose her own outfit, wore an emerald green coat and a yellow and green check dress, her long fly-away hair tied back by a large bow of emerald green ribbon. Rex, as always, was impeccably dressed in a smart grey suit with a white carnation in the button-hole. Afterwards, they all went off to the Savoy for lunch.

Once down at Withyford again, Anna rang the rectory and invited Jane Everett to a meal with, if at all possible, her husband. To her delight, she found that John Everett was having a week at home recuperating from the same sort of virus which had laid Anna so low earlier on. Although the Everetts belonged to a younger generation, the four of them got on well and Anna said she hoped they would come to Charlton Lodge sometime. With Rex beside her, she found herself becoming infinitely more sociable and lighthearted, no longer the serious grandmother, bowed down with responsibility in what she now thought of as her 'alone' days. She paid a call on Patrick Coren and his family and thanked him for the attention which she was pleased to see had been given to her father's grave. It was also gratifying to have Madge waiting on them again and to learn that her boyfriend had apparently come round to the idea of a church wedding, even if it was the wedding dress which was still uppermost in the girl's mind.

Although it was not an exactly auspicious time of year to visit Slapton Sands, nevertheless they went there again one day and stood looking out over the English Channel, seething, swirling, managing to look both grand yet menacing in the pale grey light of a winter's afternoon.

"It saved you," Rex said, "at the time of Dunkirk, and it saved the whole world later on, even if it did claim a lot of lives in doing so. I believe one of your seventeenth century sages, I think his name was Halifax, was once asked what England should do to be saved and he replied, 'Look to your moat'. The same old boy said that the best way to suppose what may come is to remember what is past."

She turned towards him, marvelling at his extraordinary knowledge of English history.

"And now they're building a channel tunnel," Rex went on. "I hope the powers that be know what they're up to. I can't help feeling that perhaps England wasn't meant to be joined on to the continent after the big bang, or whatever happened. Man is so clever now in one way, with all this technology, making the world a smaller place by air travel but . . . I don't know . . . " He broke off. Then he said, "Sorry, Anna. I suppose I've got a bee in my bonnet about it all. It's difficult to explain. But I feel we've found communism doesn't work so we've got, or are getting, rid of it. What about the common market? It sounds so awfully like the same word. Will we find that doesn't work either? Unless, of course, human nature changes but God knows when that might be."

22

SHE was shocked at Geoffrey Sheldon's appearance when she saw him sitting up in bed in a small partitioned room in a nursing home in Oxfordshire just before Christmas. Anna had written to ask if he would like a visit and was rather surprised when he had replied in the affirmative. She was afraid that the embarrassment he had apparently shown when he had to explain to Nicholas Clarke the reason for renouncing his guardianship of Chloe, might mean that he would find it difficult to maintain any further contact.

"It's good of you to come, Anna," he said, as she sat down beside him and laid an arrangement of Christmas roses on his bedside locker.

"Not at all. You were one of Steven's best friends. I'm so . . . terribly sorry, Geoffrey."

"Thank you, and for the flowers. They're lovely." He looked at her with a kind of anguished gratitude, his eyes large and dark, his cheeks sunken, a travesty of the good-looking man she had known. Had Steven ever suspected, she wondered? No, surely not. At the time of Chloe's birth, Geoffrey had been happily married, that is, to all outward appearances. But it probably hadn't been a happy marriage at all. Was Geoffrey one of those strange individuals who were AC/DC, as some people flippantly referred to them? Was that why there had never been any children, why his wife had left him, unable to keep up the façade any longer? It would probably have been incomprehensible to Steven, with all the normal male instincts, to have ever envisaged that Geoffrey wasn't entirely like himself.

The man in the bed struggled to put on a brave face. "You've married again, Anna. I'm so glad for you. How is Chloe?"

"She's well, Geoffrey. We shall all be moving to a place called Charlton Lodge near Richmond in the New Year. There are some riding stables almost next door and she's very excited. She's going to learn to ride."

He nodded. "That's nice. Steven would have been pleased."

"Yes. I think he would."

"Anna, I wanted to tell you that apart from my housekeeper and a few friends, I have no other particularly close relationships with anyone. Chloe will inherit the bulk of my estate when she's eighteen. I've made a trust fund for her, tied it all up with Nicholas Clarke."

"Oh, Geoffrey!" She found herself floundering. What did one say to such a statement? Thank you? You shouldn't have? Chloe, in any case, would be well provided for. She put out a hand in a silent gesture of gratitude, which he held in his pale emaciated one. For several minutes, they did not speak.

"I'm afraid neither Steven nor I made much of a success of marriage," he said, at length. "It's the least I can do for his daughter."

She stayed another quarter of an hour, promised to come again, and left. But as she walked along the corridor to the lift, she doubted there would be another time.

It looked as if, for Geoffrey, there was not much of it left. She went out to her car but she did not immediately start on her return journey. Chloe and Rex were going to explore the riding stables and its facilities that day. There was no need for her to hurry. She stayed where she was for a while, as the winter's afternoon closed in on her. She thought about homosexuality and her hitherto innate revulsion towards it. Now, seeing Geoffrey as he was, she simply felt chagrined and infinitely sad. She supposed it was as impossible for Geoffrey to resist his predilection for the same sex, as it had been for Lysette to resist her overindulgence in heterosexual intercourse. In Anna's conventional and, as she now felt, narrow and sanctimonious life, she had mentally blacklisted both activities. If anything, she thought today that Lysette's seemed the most unnatural and immoral. After all, she had been a mother with a small child. The trouble with you, Anna said to herself as she eventually started up the car, is that you want things too perfect and life just isn't like that, as Rex was inferring when we were last down at Slapton. It never will be and, right at the moment, you've got it as perfect as possible. So make the most of it. Stop worrying. You're luckier than you deserve, considering what a mess you made of everything when you were young.

This sentiment was reinforced when she arrived back at the hotel to find Chloe and Rex playing chess. Chloe appeared to be winning, although how much this was due to her opponent's diplomacy Anna was not sure. But what she was sure about was that, backed up by Eve Wilson, Rex had certainly worked a miracle with her granddaughter. Chloe was now taking such a different attitude towards him and, indeed, towards her and their whole new way of life.

It wasn't exactly ideal having to spend Christmas in a hotel yet, here again, it proved a great deal more enjoyable than some of the ones which Anna and Chloe had spent together in the past. Fortunately, several other children of Chloe's age happened to be spending Christmas in the hotel also, and if anyone thought it strange that the girl was in the care of an older generation, Rex and

Anna were never made to feel aware of it.

One evening, when Anna went into Chloe's bedroom to say goodnight to her, the child said, "I can't think why you didn't marry Rex all that time ago, Gran. Whatever *did* make you turn him down?" It was a question which Chloe had put to her before, but this time it was posed in a kinder manner. Looking at her granddaughter, she replied, quietly, "It's difficult to answer, Chloe. In the light of hindsight, I wonder why myself."

Yet afterwards, lying in bed beside a sleeping Rex, she thought, 'I didn't exactly turn you down. I turned you on. Deliberately.' Chloe's questions were utterly justifiable. Anna wondered when she might give her granddaughter *Aftermath* to read. So far, Chloe had shown little interest in the book itself and only superficial interest in the publicity surrounding it. Anna was well aware that, at Chloe's age, the activities of a grandparent were really only of importance if they concerned a grandchild directly, such as turning up at concerts and speech days, dressed in acceptable unembarrassing clothes and always being reliable when transportation was required.

There would, perhaps, come a time when Chloe would feel differently, look beyond such things. If she eventually read *Aftermath*, how much would she connect her grandmother's life with the fiction she had written? Of course, Anna had disguised her own story quite a bit. She had set the novel in another era, beginning with another war. There had been no boating tragedy — in any case the real one had happened after she had started the novel — and there had been no murder mystery, no child being cared for by a grandparent. There had, however, been a fairly graphic account of sexual yearnings in an age when unfortunate liaisons often resulted in an unwanted birth, and the fear of this which had been the only effective contraception. Even Rex hadn't quite appreciated how much this still held good in the 1940s. He had read the novel as a simple love story, written by a woman with whom he had fallen so desperately in love in his youth and, in old age, set out to find again.

Anna was suddenly conscious of the

book's astonishing sense of *déjà vu*. She had made the novel end happily because Dave Mason, her editor, and Tim Parker, her agent, had impressed on her the importance of this from the point of view of women readers. So far, the real story would appear to be following suit in the most uncanny way. Fictional life and true life seemed to have come together. Not for the first time did Anna wonder where ideas came from, what other power put them into certain people's minds. Had she subconsciously always thought that Rex would come back to her? Was that why she had responded, almost matter-of-factly, when he had rung the bell to her flat from the street not all that long ago, why she had simply pressed the buzzer so that he could enter the building almost as if she might have been expecting him.

She recalled Tim Parker having once told her about a theory held by many an artist, that creative work was all out there somewhere, up for grabs, merely waiting for someone to get tuned in and receptive to an idea, which he or she then proceeded to process and pass on to the public in the form of a book, a picture, a piece of music or sculpture. One was just a middle man, or woman, in fact.

'Michelangelo', she remembered Tim saying, as she drifted off to sleep, 'was simply waiting for the go-ahead on the Sistine Chapel'.

23

TOWARDS the end of January the real life script was certainly working out in a very different manner from the fictional *Aftermath*. In Anna's novel, movies had scarcely been invented. In 1992 it was quite another matter.

Tim Parker rang her up to say that a Mr Arnold G. Zeckendorf was interested in acquiring the film rights of *Aftermath* and could they all have lunch together. Arnold Zeckendorf was apparently only over from the States for a short time. Would that Friday, the day after tomorrow, suit Anna?

Would it, indeed. "But I'd like you to come too," she said to Rex.

"No, darling. This is your show. I'm delighted about it. I shall simply look forward to a detailed account of this mogul's proposals when you get back. Incidentally, being a Friday, I'll collect Chloe from Atherstone that afternoon."

In her excitement, Anna was mortified to realise she had forgotten about this.

She wore her wedding outfit and could not help being pleased to notice a few admiring glances as she entered the foyer of the Dorchester at the appointed time, praying that Tim would be there before her. It was a great relief when, to her short-sighted gaze, she saw two men rise to greet her.

Contrary to expectations, Arnold G. Zeckendorf was not the swarthy middle-aged forceful personality she had imagined him to be. He was young, pale, bespectacled and thin. Tim had not mentioned much more to her on the telephone than that he was fast gaining a reputation for films with a gentler image, distilling on to the screen human experience in a bygone age. "He captures time and place and people in a most remarkable way," Tim said. "I can quite see why he's become interested in *Aftermath*."

But over lunch, Arnold Zeckendorf proved, indirectly, to be interested not only in the novel but also in its author. Anna felt herself being drawn out, but in the most delicate and appreciative manner, recounting how she had come to write the book and telling Arnold things she had never even told Rex.

"You would not be too against my changing the ending slightly, would you, Anna?" — they had got on to Christian names almost at once — "making it not quite so . . . neat?"

She hesitated and looked at Tim. It was Tim and Dave Mason who had advised her to make it a happy one. Now, all he said was, "It's nice of Arnold to ask, Anna. Mostly, once the rights are sold, a producer feels he has the *perfect* right to produce something which the author of the original story can hardly recognise."

But her innate caution made her enquire, "How would you want to do this?"

Arnold waved away the sweet trolley. It was plain he was at work now, intense, utterly dedicated, his pale cheeks slightly pink, his eyes, behind their huge spectacles, piercing and animated.

"I would prefer that the two chief protagonists, Alice and Lionel, never meet up again."

She frowned as she looked once more at Tim for support. "But . . . I can't quite see . . . I mean, I understood that the public rather expect happy endings."

"The reading public, maybe. Especially women. But with films it's a bit different. We're catering for all sorts."

"But what do you propose to do with the lovers?"

Arnold sat back, held up both arms and then crossed them in the air. "Ships that pass in the night," he replied, enigmatically — and then all three of them laughed.

Recounting her experiences to Rex later that evening, he, too, roared with laughter. "I see, darling. I would be landing at Southampton while you would be boarding some fated ship like the *Titanic*. God knows how Arnold G. is going to shoot that one, but he sounds a good chap. I hope you signed whatever was necessary."

"Not yet. Tim's got to work it all out. These things take time. He warned me not to get too excited. There's many a slip, as they say."

"Of course. But just fancy. I envisaged

all sorts of scenarios about meeting you again, but never that you'd be quite so famous."

"I'm not. I've only written one novel, which may, or may not, be filmed."

"I would put my money on the affirmative."

They moved into Charlton Lodge at the end of February and the contract for the film rights of *Aftermath* was signed shortly afterwards. Tim was their first visitor, driving out from London bearing a bottle of champagne and sitting on an upturned packing case while the three of them drank it out of the only containers available: plastic mugs.

Anna, happier than she had ever been, almost had to keep pinching herself to realise her good fortune. But, with her customary good sense and discipline — and always with Rex's approval — she set about turning Charlton Lodge into her idea of a dream home. Chloe, returning from Atherstone each weekend, spent as many hours as possible at the riding stables. Having now turned eleven, she was allowed to go and come alone, although Anna was always relieved to hear her letting herself in to the back door, ever fearful of accidents, both equestrian and, indeed, pedestrian, even though the child had only one minor road to cross.

One Saturday afternoon, Anna was altering some curtains for what Rex insisted on calling her study, he himself was paying a visit to the Imperial War Museum and Chloe, as usual, was at the riding stables, when the front door bell rang. Anna went to answer it with no other thought in her mind than the hope that the caller would not hinder her too much in her current self-appointed task.

Martina Le Page and a man were standing on the step.

"*Chère Madame*," Martina began. "Forgive me for arriving so unexpectedly. But the owners of your flat told me you had remarried and gave me your address. I always felt sorry that our last meeting ended somewhat abruptly. I, too, have married again and I so much want to introduce you to my new husband, Pierre Hervouët, the present owner of the *Princess Hélène*, about whom we spoke."

The man who had not taken Lysette and Steven out on their fatal last boating trip, held out his hand. Oddly enough, he was exactly like the character Anna had imagined Arnold Zeckendorf to be before she met him: swarthy, fat and somehow slightly sinister.

"Enchanté, Madame." He bowed and, to Anna's horror, raised her hand to his lips. She recoiled and was aware that Martina, if not Pierre Hervouët, had noticed. It seemed impossible to refuse them entry. In any case, by some strange manipulative feat, they seemed to have already crossed the threshold and were standing in the hall, the woman, chic, hard-eyed and heavily scented; the man, his darting eyes beneath their bushy brows, busily taking stock of what was obviously, at the very least, a well-appointed home.

Anna led them into the drawing-room. Faced with this sudden and potentially ominous situation, she did her best, but her basically hospitable nature was firmly put to one side. She wanted to get this unfortunate meeting over and done with as soon as possible, particularly as the afternoons were still short and Chloe would soon be back from the riding stables. She was about to ask her visitors the real reason for their call, when Martina forestalled her.

"I believe you are alone, *Madame*?"

"I am. But not for long." It occurred to Anna that Martina and Pierre had probably been watching the house, had seen both Rex and Chloe leave. But she refused to let fear take hold. "What else is it which you evidently wish to say to me in private?"

The man and woman exchanged glances. Then the latter said, "*Madame*, as you know, I was Lysette's best friend. Pierre here has just obtained irrefutable evidence that your daughter-in-law's death was no accident. In order to be ready for the coming season, we have borrowed a lot of money to re-equip and modernise the *Princess Hélène*. I fear it has all cost a great deal more than estimated. We have even had the old bunk beds taken out and new, more comfortable ones installed."

"Yes?" Anna noted the reference to money and saw the man starting to pull an envelope from his pocket, from which he extracted a long broken gold chain and a separate gold cross, one she would have recognised anywhere.

"Both had slipped down behind the fixed lower bunk, *Madame*," he said. "I think you will agree that the chain must have been severed by extreme force. It has no clasp."

Anna did not take the proffered 'evidence', which was being held out to her. She simply looked at it, remembering only too well that no matter what Lysette wore, the long chain, bearing the distinctive cross, was always doubled round her neck.

She stood up, feeling slightly sick. She knew she was being blackmailed before Martina actually spoke. As if from a long way off she heard her saying, "I am sure with your devotion to your granddaughter you would never want her to know . . . "

Suddenly, the door flew open and Chloe stood there, mud from head to foot, listening wide-eyed, as Martina was ending, "that her father killed her mother."

24

IF Chloe had been younger, Anna thought she might have been able to temporize in some way. As it was, there was no question of that. Chloe was a bright, but now utterly shattered, eleven-year-old, who had also just been physically shaken up by a fall from her pony. The only benefit — if such it could be called — to be salvaged from the whole horrendous afternoon, was the fact that Martina had scuppered any chance of blackmail. The child, by appearing so unexpectedly, had been made aware, in the most brutal fashion, of how her mother had supposedly met her death. Martina and her husband — if Pierre *was* her husband — had inadvertently burnt their boats.

Afterwards, Anna was unaware of the exact sequence of events, only that the unwelcome visitors must have let themselves out, that she had put an arm around Chloe and got her upstairs to bed, where the child lay white and trembling while she telephoned for the doctor who, mercifully considering it was a weekend, came at once. Then, at last, there was the sound of Rex's voice calling up from the hall.

"Hello! Where is everyone?"

Anna came out on to the landing.

"Chloe's in bed, Rex. She's had a fall from her pony."

He was already half way up the stairs, as she started down to meet him, a finger to her lips. "She's all right. Nothing broken. But there's been . . . other trouble. The doctor's given her a sedative."

"What other trouble?" He looked bewildered and she drew him into their own bedroom and told him all that had happened.

"The bastards!" He paced up and down. "If only I'd been here." She had never seen him so angry.

"But it mightn't have stopped anything."

"Yes it might. I could have sent the bloody woman and her man packing."

"But Rex, it all happened so quickly. They were intent on making trouble.

And they succeeded, even if they left empty-handed, as it were."

"What," he asked, "did you tell the doctor?"

"That Chloe had had a fall, but that she had also just received some unfortunate news concerning her late parents."

"Did he ask what?"

"No. He was just sympathetic and tactful."

"What are you going to say to Chloe when the sedative's worn off?"

"I'm trying to think."

What could she say? What *should* she say to an orphaned eleven-year-old, who had looked on her father as some sort of hero?

Amazingly, in the end, it was Chloe herself who helped. The next morning she said to Anna, who had scarcely slept a wink all night, "Gran, I always knew there was some kind of mystery about my mother. I mean, you never wanted to talk about her, so I didn't like to either. I suppose that was one of the reasons why I wanted to go to France so much with Madame Le Page. I thought she'd tell me things that you wouldn't."

"Yes, dear. I understand."

"Did *you* know how my mother died?"

"No. No one really knows, Chloe," Anna answered, without hesitation.

"But what do you *think*, Gran?"

Anna had been waiting for the question. Suddenly as if heaven-sent, the answer came to her. "I think, Chloe, that maybe a quarrel got out of hand. I believe your father was a man who loved too much, both you and your mother."

"Can one do that?"

"Yes. Sometimes."

"You mean he loved my mother more than she loved him?"

"Yes."

The child was silent for a while. Then, somewhat surprisingly, she said, "You and Rex love each other equally, don't you?"

Anna could not help smiling. "Well, I suppose so. I hope so."

Chloe went back to her parents. "So, my father was . . . jealous. I mean, he wouldn't have meant to harm my mother, would he?"

"No. Of course not."

"So it was all a terrible mistake?"

"Yes."

"And she went overboard! How awful it must have been for him."

"Yes. Awful."

Anna noted that the child was still championing her father. The conversation was easier than she had dared to hope for. *Of course* it was a mistake. Steven would never have set out intentionally to kill his wife. He may have been determined to confront her about her infidelity. But that was quite another matter. It would certainly have accounted for Steven wanting the two of them to go out alone on the boat, as Martina had alleged at their first meeting. Although Pierre just might have made that up later. Anna would not put it past either the man or the woman to say anything if it suited them. Yet what couldn't be made up was the actual discovery of the broken chain. It had undoubtedly been Lysette's. The cross, with its pearl inlay, was unique. Anna had always noticed it whenever she had seen her daughter-in-law. Yet whatever had or had not happened on the *Princess Hélène* on that fateful day, Anna was resolved, like Chloe, to think of it as something which was never intended.

She kept the child home from school the following week, giving her fall as the reason, although Anna knew that she would have to talk to Eve Wilson soon about the far more serious one. Ten days later, when Chloe was back at Atherstone, she telephoned to ask Eve to dinner and was grateful when, in spite of her busy life, Eve agreed to an early date. "Although I've been longing to show you Charlton Lodge," Anna admitted towards the end of their conversation, "I'm afraid, sadly, I do have an ulterior motive."

"Chloe?"

"Yes."

"I understand. The child has already spoken to me."

"She *has*?"

"Yes. We've had another long discussion all about love and sex."

"What?"

"Anna, Chloe is already emotionally grown up beyond her years. I think I've mentioned before that you have a remarkably intelligent, if headstrong, granddaughter. I only hope that I can help to steer her in the right direction."

After they said goodbye, Anna sat for a long time looking out over the garden, now showing every sign of new life. The daffodils were out, the cherry blossom beginning to follow suit. The grass had already had one cutting, something which Rex insisted on doing, even though they employed a part-time gardener. She was pleased to see that the previously straight flagstone path, which she had managed to get turned into a curve, was looking much more natural. Soon the border of pinks and pansies on either side would make it even better. Yet, after talking to Eve, who was so much more experienced in the ways of present-day youth, she felt not only depressed, but redundant. The words of Lewis Carroll came back to her again with greater force: *You are old, Anna Harman* . . . You've done your best, she said to herself, as she got up to make some tea, but now others can do better. Maybe, God willing, for a few more years you and Rex can give Chloe a secure background but, whatever happens, she will have to make her own way early on in life. She's coped with the latest developments admirably, much better, in fact, than you and Rex.

Of the three of them, Anna reflected, as she waited for the kettle to boil, Rex appeared to have taken the situation worst. He kept blaming himself for having gone up to the Imperial War Museum that day. He slept badly. He put in unnecessarily long hours in the garden. He did not play golf. His research work seemed to have been abandoned. A certain fear gripped Anna, not this time for Chloe but for their marriage. She had piled nothing but trouble on him. Could he be regretting their reunion and now their union? Might she not be 'bad news', as she believed the younger generation described someone who was a moloch at the feast?

Yet, when she hinted at this, his sudden surge of passion quelled all her doubts.

25

TIM rang up during the Easter holidays to ask if he could call in on his way back from Sussex. Anna immediately invited him to lunch. She had always sensed that, although he led a busy life which brought him in to constant contact with a wide variety of people, he was basically a lonely man. Apart from the fact that he was divorced, she knew little about his private life.

She should, she knew, have asked him to come and see them again weeks ago, but had held back because she was afraid of what he might ask her. Now, almost as soon as he had settled down with a pre-prandial drink, he came straight out with the question she had been dreading.

"Your next book, Anna. It's some time since *Aftermath* was published. You told me way back that you had started another one. How's it going?"

"Oh, *Tim*. It isn't."

"It's my fault," Rex broke in. "Marrying

her and moving here has taken up all her time, but I'm doing my best to make her go on."

"But she says she isn't!" He turned back to Anna. "I'm sorry to sound like a slave driver, but we don't want too long a gap."

"Yes. I understand."

"Neither your publishers nor I think you're a one-book author. We're sure of that. Several people lately have asked me what you were doing."

She hedged. "Perhaps I've just been skiving."

Tim looked at Rex again. "Can't you lock her up somewhere? Not let her out until she's done so many words each day? I thought there was going to be a study at the top of the house."

"Yes. There is, and I've already hinted at doing just what you suggest. You shall see it after lunch," Rex replied.

There was a sudden shout from Chloe who was meant to be watching the vegetables cooking in the kitchen. With relief, Anna said, "Excuse me," and went out of the room, leaving the two men together.

As she began dishing up, Anna felt she hadn't been quite fair to Tim. Certainly, she had had plenty to keep her occupied. There had been Rex's amazing re-emergence into her life, her illness, marriage and moving house. But he didn't know about the Martina affair and how much it had troubled her. Although how could he? She couldn't possibly tell him, any more than she could mention another far more pleasant excuse: that, with Martina out of the picture she was happy, happier than she had ever been. There was no need to counteract loneliness by outpourings on paper. She was fulfilled in a way she had never imagined possible. She would have been willing to type Rex's indecipherable longhand, if he had allowed her to do so. But he had said, "For God's sake, Anna. Let me retain a little self-respect. What I am doing is simply recording. It interests me, but it may not interest anyone else. That remains to be seen. But I have no talent whatsoever for creative work."

The subject of her creative work did not come up again until she showed Tim over the house just before he left.

"You won't forget, will you?" he said, as he eyed her abandoned typewriter. "It would be good to feel there was another Anna Linsdale book coming along."

She promised she would do her best, but after he had gone she doubted her ability, or even inclination to continue writing. *Aftermath* had been what she believed the younger generation called a 'one off'. The story had come to her out of the blue, it had brought Rex back to her, almost as if that had been ordained. It had fulfilled its purpose.

Anna tried not to give in to fanciful ideas, but when she looked round at Charlton Lodge that afternoon, saw Chloe setting off for the riding stables — her fall appeared to have had no lasting effect on her equestrian enthusiasm — noticed Rex getting out the lawn mower as she began stacking the dishwasher, it seemed as if what she had now was enough, more than enough, more than she deserved.

Yet, mindful of her promise to Tim, later that evening she went up to her so-called study and pulled out some pages of manuscript which she had hidden in a drawer. On reading them, they gave her little satisfaction. She had an eerie feeling that she was no longer in touch with whoever or whatever had prompted her to write *Aftermath*. All she really wanted to do now was to watch Chloe growing up and enjoy the remaining years she and Rex might have left to them.

But even as she sat with the folder pushed to one side of the desk, knowing that she would never continue with its contents, the words *The Remaining Years* seemed to dance in front of her. They would make a good title, a good title for a sequel, a sequel to *Aftermath*. She did at least have first hand knowledge of love in later life, love which was disbelieved or discredited or even laughed at by younger generations. Almost roughly, she pulled her small typewriter towards her and set out THE REMAINING YEARS. The bold black capitals stared up at her, almost like a challenge.

Of course, it wouldn't be a book of which Arnold G. Zeckendorf would approve, with his desire for none-too-happy endings. But what did that matter?

It was nothing to do with him. He had got what he wanted, with no late flowering romance to interfere with the ending to his film. She could quite see now why he wanted *Aftermath* to finish his way. He was so *young*. He didn't want two old fuddy-duddys making fools of themselves. Well, good luck to him.

Yet Anna couldn't help feeling a twinge of guilt at how easily she had acquiesced to his altering her story. She felt as if she had somehow betrayed the characters. They had been so real to her while she was writing about them. And still were, for that matter. Tim had said that Arnold was planning to come over to England again in the summer and look for likely locations in which to shoot the film. Naturally, the West Country would be high on the agenda. Perhaps she and Rex might pay another visit to Withyford then. Take Chloe with them. There would surely be riding stables in the vicinity. She would get on to the Everetts. It would be good to see them again. Then she had second thoughts. *Aftermath* no longer belonged to her. Perhaps it really was best to get on with something else.

She wondered why the words *The Remaining Years* had suddenly come into her head and appealed to her so much. Could it be because she remembered her father had once preached something in one of his sermons about the importance of picking up the remains. 'When disaster strikes', he had said, 'you must pick up the remains. It is astonishing how many you will find'. He was, of course, referring to the Sermon on the Mount: *Gather up the fragments that remain, that nothing be lost.*

That nothing be lost. She sat thinking about loss for a while: the loss of her father, of deliberately losing Rex as a young man, the loss of her husband — however unsatisfactory a one he had been — of the tragic loss of her son and even of Geoffrey Sheldon, who was not expected to live much longer. Then, into her mind came the thought of all those anonymous losses in the Second World War, especially the ones at Slapton Sands into which Rex was putting so much research. She sent up a small prayer of thankfulness for what she had left: an older Rex and a youthful Chloe. She began to type, slowly at first and then with increasing urgency, as she began picking up the remains.

26

ANNA wrote hard that summer — and fast. Sometimes she was amazed at how quickly *The Remaining Years* began to take shape. Rex was delighted, but she did not show him any of the manuscript, partly because she had always thought that if anyone praised her unfinished work she would hardly believe them and, if there were criticisms, then she might be too discouraged to go on. Not that she felt Rex would be likely to criticise.

But she had yet another reason for keeping this novel strictly private during its execution. She was not writing about people being apart from each other, but together. There was a lot of herself in it, far more than in *Aftermath*. Sometimes she wondered if she could ever bring herself to show it to anyone. She only knew that it had to be written and that it was more or less writing itself. The characters were so real, so forceful.

Often, they seemed so contrary that it was quite difficult to make them behave as she wanted.

Anna recalled one evening during the Second World War when she had joined a group of others to play *Planchette* in the Nurses' Home. The game had fascinated her, although touching on the occult as it did, she felt that her parents would hardly have approved of it. Someone round the table had asked if there was anyone wanting to talk to one or the other of them — and the upturned glass, with all their forefingers pressed on it, virtually flew to the letters K. I. N. G. No one seemed to know anyone personally of that name and then Anna suddenly thought: KING = REX, and had made an excuse to leave the table.

Now, all these years later, she still felt she might have been playing *Planchette* on her typewriter. Her fingers, like that glass, flitted along the keys almost as if motivated by some unseen force. She marvelled at how, without warning, she had begun to write again. Only at weekends, when Chloe was home, did she make a determined effort to break off although, even then, if the child were riding and Rex perhaps playing golf, she would sneak up to her study and put in the odd hour.

During the week, she thanked God that Rex, far from feeling excluded, rejoiced in what he called the revisitation of her muse. 'I will cook tonight', he would say firmly, and sometimes she would feel desperately guilty, on coming down to the kitchen to find him concentrating on some unusual dish which she had never thought to tackle herself.

Then, while it was in the oven, they would have a drink, outside on the patio if possible, talking little, as always simply content to be in each other's company. One evening Rex said, "At the rate you're going, Anna, when do you think the book will be finished?"

She hesitated. They were almost into July. Soon, Chloe would be home for the summer holidays. She realised that, apart from feeling unable to let up, she had probably been hoping, subconsciously, that she might have finished *The Remaining Years* by then. But she knew now, it was an impossibility.

"Maybe mid-August," she answered, hopefully.

"That's fine. Then don't you think it would be a good idea for us all to take a break? We could do a bit of touring. That new car I bought is crying out to be used rather more. Why don't we let it take us where it will?"

"You mean in England?"

"Where else? We could show Chloe Withyford and maybe Slapton, and then just go on from there."

It seemed incredible that he was suggesting something which had already come into her mind. Whether or not they saw Arnold Zeckendorf was neither here nor there. She became filled with enthusiasm, the tiredness which she had begun to feel at the end of each day suddenly lifted, even before the reviving drink Rex had put into her hand had had time to take effect.

Although they employed good regular daily help, Anna was aware that she tired much more quickly these days, that she could no longer do the things which, a decade ago, she knew she would have been able to manage quite easily. Once upon a time, she had felt it might have been better to keep Chloe at day school. Now, she was thankful that Dr Fenton had persuaded her to opt for weekly boarding. Of course, neither of them could have envisaged Rex coming into the picture, that her life would alter so much. The past year had been like a revolution, a pleasant revolution if the adjective could be applied to such a noun. But revolutions, pleasant or unpleasant, could be exhausting. She was sad that, owing to her move, Dr Fenton was no longer her GP. It would have been nice to talk to him about it all, yet her new one had been more than helpful and solicitous, especially over Chloe's accident.

Although the thought of their proposed touring holiday spurred Anna on to greater efforts until Chloe broke up, she became more aware that her exhaustion was increasing. She did her best to hide the fact from Rex but, one evening after he had taken her out to dinner to celebrate her seventieth birthday, as they were driving home through Richmond Park, he said, "Anna, it isn't all that necessary to finish your novel before we go away, is it?"

"No," she answered, truthfully. "I don't really know why I thought it was."

"Then why not ease up? I think you're overdoing it. I shouldn't have encouraged you so much. When Chloe comes home for the holidays next week, why not give it a rest?"

So, he *had* noticed. Nothing escaped Rex. She would have to be more careful.

He drove slowly through the park, much more slowly than the official speed limit. Then he stopped the car altogether and, as if by mutual consent, they got out and walked, hand in hand, to a small clump of trees where they sat down. The long light evening seemed to envelope them. She thought of another such a one, half a century ago, when she had been almost crying out with desire for him to make love to her. Tonight, she was simply grateful for something much more important: just his love and the empathy between them, reinforced by the way that so often they found that they were thinking about the same thing.

She was not in the least surprised when, as he put an arm round her, he remarked, "That funny old woman coming towards us with her dog, could well be Lizzie Maidment."

She laughed. "Though hardly interrupting any doubtful goings-on."

The walker passed on by, without giving them a second glance.

But on the way home she thought of how Rex had referred to the woman as 'old'. Anna realised that, at the time Lizzie Maidment had broken in on their love-making she had probably been only about forty, thirty years younger than Anna was now. Lizzie had probably been dead some time. She would never have known what a fateful part she had played in Anna's life.

Fate. It was a word which had always fascinated Anna ever since her school days. She recalled it had been the subject of an essay her form had been asked to write during her final term. The English mistress had chalked up three quotations on the blackboard for them to consider. Anna had opted for the last, a line from a seventeenth century poet, James Shirley.

It came back to her now with unusual clarity: *There is no armour against fate.*

As they got out of the car when they arrived at Charlton Lodge, she shivered slightly, as if someone had walked over her grave.

27

WHEN the Everetts heard that there was a chance of Anna, Rex and Chloe coming to Withyford that August, they insisted that they must all stay at the rectory. "It'll be holiday time for everyone," Jane said, "and, believe it or not, there's going to be a gymkhana in Hawker's Field. You told me in your last letter how keen Chloe was on riding."

Anna had kept up with the Everetts since they had first met and had always given them an open invitation to visit Charlton Lodge but, as yet, this had not come about. She felt slightly guilty that, lately, because she had been working so hard, she had not pressed the point; and the spontaneity with which Jane was now urging them to stay at the rectory was almost embarrassing.

"The hospitality is so one-sided," she parried, remembering, also, the lovely cut glass rose bowl the Everetts had given them when they came down to Withyford after their marriage.

"Rubbish! The pleasure will be ours," Jane replied, "but I promise later in the year we'll really come to you. But, just now, think how lovely it will be for our twins to have your Chloe for company. I'll ask the local riding stables for a good safe pony for her, say about thirteen hands?"

There was no demurring now. Anna knew that Chloe would be ecstatic when she heard. She came away from the telephone pleased and grateful that Jane Everett appeared to find nothing extraordinary in a rapport between herself, the mother of ten-year-old twins, and Anna, a recently remarried grandmother of an eleven-year-old granddaughter.

The gymkhana was to be on Saturday, the fifteenth, and Jane had suggested that they should come at least two or three days before in order for Chloe to get used to her new mount. Anna's mind went back to the 1930s, when Hawker's Field had belonged to a farming family by that name. Was there still a Hawker who owned it? Or had Hawker's Field simply stuck, so that later generations referred to it by its original nomenclature without in the least knowing — or even bothering to know — why. She recalled that sometimes, when on leave during the war, she had helped the Hawkers at haymaking time, driving a tractor and sweep. Once, she had turned too quickly and had run the sweep into a fence. Mortified, she had expected righteous anger from Fred Hawker, but had been vastly relieved by the humorous and tolerant way he had accepted the situation. With hindsight, she realised that the daughter of the rector was looked upon kindly by the village community with the exception, perhaps, of Lizzie Maidment.

With the thought of Chloe, her granddaughter, soon to compete for a rosette in Hawker's Field, Anna found herself thinking more and more about her own roots. Why had she not learned to ride in the 1930s? Had it been a question of money? Or her mother's automatic antipathy to any form of pleasure? Or simply indifference, something of which Anna herself now felt guilty, when she remembered how Chloe had evidently been silently longing to ride and how much the activity now meant to her.

It would be good to give the child a treat like this and a chance to stay in her grandmother's old home. She wondered which bedrooms they would be given. She was sure they would be comfortable, very different from the spartan hard-bedded ones she remembered, with the only bathroom and lavatory miles down a passage, the latter with a wide wooden seat, cut-up newspapers instead of toilet rolls and cold linoleum striking a chill to slipperless feet on even the hottest day.

Anna wondered whether Madge Musselwhite would still be waitressing at the Withyford Arms or whether she had given notice, having married in the white wedding dress she so hankered after. They would be sure to find out because both she and Rex were determined to entertain the Everetts there as much as possible during their stay. Somehow, Anna did not think she would bother to look up Della again. Judging from the reception she received last time she would hardly be welcome. That was a chapter best left closed.

As Anna had anticipated, Chloe was thrilled at the prospect of riding in the Withyford gymkhana and spent every conceivable minute during the first part of her holidays in a field at the back of the stables, practising for various events. The management had kindly arranged for a low post and rails to be erected, as well as sticks spaced just the right distance apart for bending through, and even a bucket and posts for a mock potato race.

"I do wish I could take Diamond to Withyford," Chloe said one evening, after Rex and Anna had come out to watch her progress and they were all walking home.

"But I'm sure Mrs Everett will get you just as good a pony," Rex replied.

"Yes, but that's not the point. I won't have *practised* on it."

Her fierce competitiveness amused Rex, but somewhat alarmed Anna. She glanced at the child's flushed excited face after all her recent exertions. She was going to be beautiful all right. Another six years or so, would she break some man's heart, as

Lysette had broken Steven's? Presumably, Chloe wouldn't have to suffer from all the sexual inhibitions and fears which had beset Anna. It was all so different now. Life in those days seemed inexplicable to her granddaughter. Anna had tried more than once lately to tell Chloe about the rectory as it had been in her youth, but had met with, if not exactly inattentiveness, certainly blank astonishment.

"No central heating?" the child had said and Anna had replied, "No, and, of course, later on there was a war when the cold seemed even worse." "Oh," came the query, "I suppose you wore masses of clothes in winter, a couple of pairs of tights, perhaps?" "There *were* no tights in those days," Anna answered, almost annoyed at her granddaughter's ignorance. "Then how on earth . . . ?" Chloe began and her grandmother cut her short. "We had stockings and suspender belts, my dear, and woe betide anyone who was seen climbing a rope in the gym at school and showed a gap between the tops of her stockings and the bottoms of her knickers. 'Smiles' they were called."

"Good heavens," Chloe had interjected, "I'm glad I didn't live then." "But there were compensations," Anna went on. Yet, without a rejoinder, the conversation lapsed.

Later that night, Anna had wondered what exactly were the compensations. Life had been slower, certainly, and the young had been both more restricted yet more free. Even under Janet's hawk-like supervision, at Chloe's age she could wander up to the woods above Withyford, admittedly usually with a friend, sometimes picking primroses with which to decorate the church for Easter or, later on, collecting berries and autumnal leaves for harvest festival. Anna could recall kneeling on the cold damp stone floor round the font, immensely proud of her artistic floral arrangements. Sadly, she thought of how little, later on, she had bothered to contribute to church affairs, how, during the war when she had been at home it had been hard to suppress her unwillingness to attend a service. Often, she must have disappointed her father. And only last year, she knew that she had initially not been particularly affable to the latest incumbent — Madge's 'all beard and glasses' man — and because of this had sent him, when she got home, an even larger cheque towards the church funds and the upkeep of her father's grave.

Did one only learn with age? To be kinder? More tolerant? To try to make up for past failures and omissions? There had been many a time, Anna now realised, when she simply hadn't thought about how her actions might affect others. It was all very well for Rex to say that she had seemed to spend her life caring for them. But it wasn't true. How much had she thought about *his* feelings all those years ago and how her heartless rejection might have affected him? She had been far too keen protecting Number One, the holier-than-thou rector's daughter.

Even now, for several weeks she had still been putting this curious idiosyncratic desire to write in front of everything, however much Rex had appeared to encourage her. It didn't matter, *of course* it didn't matter, whether *The Remaining Years* got finished this year, next year or never. What counted was the present and the love she had never expected to find.

From now on, she would put her all into making the very best of their forthcoming holiday.

28

CONTRARY to the tricks of memory which usually made any place that was re-visited in later life seem much smaller than it used to be, Anna found Hawker's Field rather larger than she recalled. On inspecting it with Chloe, Belinda and Rose on the evening of their arrival in Withyford, she was surprised to find two separate rings had been cordoned off, one for the more ordinary gymkhana events, the other for jumping.

All three children were determined to enter for as many competitions as possible in their particular age group and, during the next forty-eight hours, they were hardly seen at the rectory, having persuaded one or another of the grown-ups to drive them to the local stables from which Jane had hired Chloe's mount, a good-looking pony of rather more than thirteen hands, called Minker. From what Anna could see of their respective horsemanship, it was obvious that Chloe, admittedly slightly older, was also a much more accomplished rider than the twins. Yet, far from being jealous, they seemed to regard her with awe, almost amounting to hero or, rather, heroine worship. Chloe took Minker in and out of some practice bending sticks with such expertise that the child confided in Anna later on that the pony proved to be far easier to handle than Diamond.

As the deadline for the gymkhana drew nearer, the excitement at the rectory became almost tangible. The weather that Saturday morning was all everyone had been hoping for and the children, for once made to stay home, spent the time in and out of the swimming-pool under the supervision of John and Rex, while Anna helped Jane indoors, where she was preparing for a barbecue that evening. Her energy, efficiency and cheerfulness were infectious and the variety of labour-saving devices which she had installed in her kitchen made Anna's own domestic improvements at Charlton Lodge seem quite inadequate and she said as much. "Although I suppose," she added, with a laugh, "my kitchen is rather better than how I remember this one."

"And how *do* you remember it?" came her hostess's interested question.

Anna had a sudden vision of washing days, of her mother coping with coarse unwieldly sides-to-middle sheets during the war when, perhaps, a Mrs Hapgood or Musselwhite or Shergold had failed to turn up, of Janet's swollen red hands as she wielded a plunger once she had got all the 'whites' into the copper, and the creaking of the mangle as those same hands manoeuvred the various items through it: her father's surplices always seeming to emerge first, taking priority over the more mundane articles. 'Peg these out on the line, will you, Anna?' she could hear Janet saying, 'there's a funeral tomorrow'.

How could she explain, Anna wondered, to this charming young housewife, living at the end of the twentieth century, what Monday mornings were like fifty or sixty years ago at Withyford rectory? One had to experience them, watch the steam clouding the windows or maybe listen to Mrs Shergold's muttered curses if it were raining. When it was, one gradually became aware of that indefinable wet-woollen-clothes-hanging-up-to-dry smell, which seemed to permeate the whole of the indoors, and one tried to avoid the back regions as far as possible, for fear of being slapped in the face by a wet sheet hanging from the wooden rack which had been hoisted up to the ceiling.

"It was all so *hard*," Anna said, at length. "Hard labour, hard water, hard soap, even. Square yellow blocks of it. None of those lovely washing powders as advertised on T.V., which nowadays make everything whiter-than-white. Although I reckon no one could have looked more snowy or pristine than my dear late father when he was officiating at a service. Only the other day, I was telling some young girl that when I first came to live alone in a London flat I didn't actually have a washing-machine, because I sent my sheets to the laundry and did my own personal washing. And this nice little thing said, 'But how?' All I could do was to put out my hands and mime a kind of washing gesture and she stared at me as if I were not quite all there. But, seriously, I simply can't recognise the place we're sitting in now. Your enormous fridge and deep freeze in that alcove are where, I suppose, the coal range used to be and that tumble-drier in our old scullery was something unheard-of in my mother's day, as I suppose mangles and coppers are rarely heard of now."

"Were people happier then, do you think?" Jane asked, speculatively.

Anna thought for a moment. Her mother certainly wasn't, but then Janet had had personal emotional problems. Would every modern convenience have made them any better? Hardly. But perhaps, in the end, it all came down to basic personality. Jane, with her undoubted plethora of material goods, was a happy person. She had created a happy home. Another woman, with just the same assets, might not be.

"I think," Anna answered, "it was probably a bit like now. Some people were happier. Some weren't. Although I can't help thinking if you and I were suddenly shunted back into a 1930s kitchen, we might just have something to say about it!"

Jane and Anna's morning, with its pleasant interchange of thought and experience, seemed to fly by, although not as fast as the aspiring equestriennes could have hoped. After an early lunch, long before two o'clock, they were in Hawker's Field, checking girths, adjusting stirrups and lining up to submit their names and entry fees. The minor events took place first in the smaller enclosure and, amidst much merriment and applause, Chloe romped home ahead of the others so many times that Anna felt both embarrassed and highly relieved when the twins won the wheelbarrow race and Belinda came second in the egg and spoon.

Then the more serious business of the afternoon began and the spectators moved away to spread themselves around the jumping ring. The junior competitors started the proceedings, negotiating easily detachable post and rails and little white gates, the higher ones being reserved for the more mature entrants. Once again, Chloe starred. Having tied for first place with another competitor, both of them having ridden clear rounds, they were obliged to repeat the performance, Chloe losing by one point. Afterwards, she walked over to watch the senior jumping with the rectory party and was plainly put out by her failure, although both Anna and Rex privately thought the experience salutary.

Before the prizes were distributed, somewhat to everyone's surprise, a long trestle table was brought into the ring, on which were placed some cups and saucers and plates. It was then given out over the loud speaker that Miss Gabrielle Houghton, the outstanding winner of the senior jumping, would end the afternoon's proceedings with a short display. Chloe immediately perked up. Her eyes never left the rider as, once again, Gabrielle rode a faultless round over jumps which had been made fractionally higher. Then, to the astonishment of the crowd, the girl took her horse to one end of the ring, turned and raced towards the mock tea table, which she cleared in such spectacular fashion that the applause was deafening.

Anna shot a quick glance at Chloe. Her face was a picture. It was as if the child had been transported. Then, all the competitors were called back into the ring, where they paraded round on their mounts while a stout lady and a gentleman wearing a monocle — 'the local squirearchy', Jane whispered — distributed the silver cups and rosettes.

Afterwards, everything happened so quickly that Anna could never remember properly exactly what took place. She seemed to recall turning away from the ring, intent on finding the owner of the riding stables to settle up with him for the hire of Minker — something Anna had insisted on doing, though much against Jane's wishes — because she, Rex and Chloe would be leaving the rectory next day. There was then a sudden curious sound from the crowd, a kind of muffled gasp of astonishment as the flying figure of a girl on a pony cantered back into the ring and Anna saw, with horror and disbelief, Chloe on Minker — his bridle still covered with rosettes — wheeling round at one end of the ring, just as Gabrielle had done, and racing hell for leather towards the tea-table. There was no chance of stopping her. Mesmerised, Anna watched the pony, urged on by his rider, reach the unfamiliar obstacle, take off too soon and then carry table and crockery in front of him before falling sideways with Chloe underneath.

Anna ran. A lot of other people seemed to run beside her and gather round as Minker rolled off the prostrate form and Anna knelt down beside it, while another man knelt down opposite. By the quiet authoritative way he asked for an ambulance to be sent and the rest of the crowd to stand back, she knew he was a doctor.

It wasn't until the two of them were in the ambulance with Chloe, after what seemed like an hour but was, in fact, only twenty minutes, that Anna wondered vaguely where Rex was. Her mind had been too shocked to take in anything other than that Chloe was badly injured. But she was sure Rex must have been there. Perhaps he had now gone on ahead in his car and would be waiting to greet them at the hospital, probably the one which had arisen on the site of the tin-hutted emergency establishment where she had once spent so many long days — and nights — working and worrying about the young American captain with whom she had fallen so hopelessly in love.

But Rex was not at New Manor when they arrived and her concern for Chloe was such that she did not think about this for some time. She was enough of a nurse to know that the situation was serious, desperately serious, but she had no means of knowing the extent of Chloe's injuries, only that the doctor on the scene who had rendered first aid had, mercifully, seemed efficient and infinitely kind.

She was asked to wait in a small anteroom while further examinations took place. It was bright and cheerful, very different from the dreary colourless ones she had known in the past. But she was still too dumb with shock to register this. Her mind kept going over and over the events at the end of the gymkhana: Chloe on Minker racing into the ring, the terrifying spectacle of horse and rider and tea-table all coming together in a flying mass, accompanied by the sound of splitting wood, breaking china, a dull thud and the anguished cries of the crowd.

What on earth had made the girl do such a thing? Anna knew she was highly competitive, but surely failure to win the junior jumping could not have affected her to such an extent that she felt she had to compensate by making a spectacle of herself? Prove her expertise? Or was Chloe, as Eve Wilson had hinted on several occasions, wild, unpredictable, more than 'a bit of a handful'? Like her mother, in fact. Anna had accepted that she was highly strung, mercurial, apt to be up one minute and down the next. She thought of how difficult the child had been when Rex had first come on the scene and then, in no time at all, how she had altered. Anna liked to think it was Rex who had worked the miracle. But could it possibly have been what Rex had to offer? Riding? This all-consuming passion for riding? No, she would not, must not, think that. With the girl lying so ill just down the passage, it was little short of sacrilege.

Yet Anna's mind, even in its confused state, kept asking, even demanding, explanations and, as time went by, an explanation as to why she was now alone, keeping vigil. Where was Rex?

It was getting on for seven before the doctor and another man, whom Anna thought might or might not be a specialist, opened the door. She started to get up but fell back, gratefully, when he motioned her to remain seated. "You are the little girl's grandmother, I believe?" he asked, gently, and Anna nodded without speaking. "Her parents?" he queried, "are they . . . ?" This time she cut him short. "Dead," she answered, "both dead," and her voice seemed high and unnatural, so that she didn't recognise it.

Both men looked troubled. "You have bad news," she went on, more as a statement of fact than a question.

There was a small silence and then the elder man answered, "I'm afraid so. But we shall know so much more when . . . " he hesitated, "your granddaughter comes out of her coma."

29

IT was October. An afternoon sun was beginning to cast long shadows over the garden, as Anna pushed her granddaughter, in a wheel-chair, back from the summerhouse. It was exactly twelve months since Rex had come into her life again, exactly two since he had left it. Strange, or perhaps not so strange, she thought, the way she kept remembering another of her father's favourite texts for a sermon: *The Lord gave and the Lord hath taken away.* But at least we had almost a year, she said to herself. I must remember that.

The child in the chair was quiet, too quiet, Anna felt. Yet, thank God, her intelligence had not been impaired. But, all the same, Chloe was different. And who wouldn't be? Would she walk again? There was every hope, so they said. It was early days, of course, days which seemed to pass with agonising slowness since that hot mid-August one which had started with such happiness and hope.

It was Jane Everett who had eventually come to the hospital the night after the gymkhana, when Anna had been sitting by Chloe's bed. A nurse stood in the doorway and said, "There is someone to see you, Mrs Harman. I will stay with your granddaughter." And Anna had gone back into the little anteroom where she had waited before, expecting to see Rex. But it was Jane who rose to greet her. "I've brought a few overnight things," she said, indicating a small case on the floor. "For us both, actually."

"Both?"

"Yes, well, I knew you were staying and I thought . . . you might need support."

"But you can't. I mean . . . Rex?"

Jane looked away.

"Where *is* Rex?" Anna's voice had risen. "Where *is* he?" she repeated. "Why hasn't he come instead of you?" Her usually courteous manner had given way to something akin to resentment, even anger.

Jane turned back to face her. For a moment neither spoke and then the younger woman came and put her arms round the older one, saying, quietly, "Rex wanted to come, Anna, so much. He was taken ill, you see, trying to reach Chloe when she fell."

"Oh, *no*! What happened? Where *is* he . . . ?" she said again.

"We got him back to the rectory, but . . . "

"But *what*?" Anna gripped the other woman now, virtually shaking her into answering. Jane had not meant to tell Anna everything that night, but it was impossible to pretend any longer. In words that were barely audible, she replied, "He had a heart attack, Anna. In fact, I think he must have had two. We thought at first he was only winded when he tripped trying to get to Chloe and that he was going to be all right. He wanted John to drive him after the ambulance and we felt it might be the best thing, because he could get medical attention that way. He kept maintaining that there was nothing wrong. While he was waiting for John to bring the car to the front door, he said to me, 'I suppose you realise how much I love Anna. I've always loved her. I'm so grateful for the time we've just had. It's been wonderful finding her again.' Then he got up and I knew he wasn't going to make it to the car."

Anna recalled nothing more of that night. She was put to bed in another room and given an injection. The last thing she heard was Jane saying, "Don't worry. I'll sit by Chloe." Then, mercifully, oblivion took over.

How she would have got by after that without the Everetts, Anna never knew. They were constantly 'there', arranging Rex's funeral in the Withyford church, helping over Chloe's transfer to Stoke Mandeville Hospital, John quietly assisting her over business matters and Jane coming to stay with her for a whole week when Anna first went back to Charlton Lodge. Apart from her own not inconsiderable assets — especially after the sale of the film rights for *Aftermath* — Anna found she had been left a very rich woman although, in her shattered state, it was something she barely took in. Only when she was told that it might be possible to care for Chloe at home, provided she employed a trained nurse, did she suddenly start to count her blessings in that expense was no object.

Other people, too, were infinitely kind. Her daily help volunteered to stay overnight whenever the occasion warranted it. Her solicitor, Nicholas Clarke, came to see her, as did Eve Wilson and Tim. Neighbours, also, rallied round. And Jane made special arrangements to leave the twins and became a frequent visitor. Only that week she had spent twenty-four hours at Charlton Lodge. "How Chloe's improved," she kept saying and Anna had replied, "You really think so? Being with her every day, it's difficult to notice. But the specialist is sure she'll be walking again before long. Then I don't think we'll need a nurse, especially if I can arrange for some physiotherapy."

Just before she left, Jane said, "Anna, I don't quite know how to put this, but it's something John and I have talked over very seriously. We want . . . I mean . . . if, later on, it ever gets too much for you, we'd like to look after Chloe. Treat her as one of the family. We'd do our very best."

Anna stared at her. She knew, of course, what Jane was trying to get at, but had been too sensitive to come right out with it. Age. Anna was, after all, seventy. She felt too overcome to do anything other than get up and kiss this generous and gentle young mother.

"It's not just because we feel guilty, mind," Jane went on, finding it easier to speak now.

"Guilty? Why on earth should you?"

"Well, I mean, if we hadn't been so keen for you to come for the gymkhana . . . Chloe would never have had her accident. We're not likely to forget."

"You must never think like that."

"But don't you, sometimes?"

Anna's mind went back to the essay she had been asked to write in her last year at school. "Maybe I used to," she replied, guardedly. "I admit, I have sometimes thought, with hindsight, I might have acted differently and wished I had. But then I've realised that one can't, or shouldn't, try to play God. There's no armour against fate. But

Jane, my dear, you can't imagine what your offer has meant to me. It's taken such a load off my mind. I realise I'm . . . well . . . getting on."

Some time afterwards, Tim, on one of his visits, also remarked on Chloe's amazing progress. "You've dispensed with the nurse, I see," he said.

"Yes. And Chloe's a fighter, all right. I think the child is determined to do whatever she can to make up for what happened. She's subdued. More responsible. With the help of my daily who's agreed to live in and a young married woman who comes to give Chloe regular tuition each day plus a physiotherapist, we manage quite well."

"Then Anna, could I ask, does it mean . . . that you might now have time to write again? You never did tell me much about the novel you were working on in the summer."

"Didn't I? It seems such a long time ago now."

"What was it about? Did you have a title?"

"Yes. I was going to call it *The Remaining Years.*"

"That's good. How far had you got?"

"About three quarters of the way through, I suppose."

"What about tackling the last quarter?"

She shook her head. "I shan't write anything else, Tim. *Aftermath* brought Rex back to me, but I often think I should never have agreed to let Zeckendorf alter the end. I suppose it's fanciful of me, but I've sometimes even thought of just retribution. I don't feel that one should play around with fiction any more than one should play around with life. And perhaps one should never put too much of oneself into a novel. I know that *The Remaining Years* was far too personal. Although, of course, actually there were no remaining years. Less than one, in fact."

"You wouldn't let me see the manuscript, would you?"

Again she shook her head. "It wouldn't be possible, Tim. You see, I tore it up."

Other titles in the
Ulverscroft Large Print Series:

TO FIGHT THE WILD
Rod Ansell and Rachel Percy

Lost in uncharted Australian bush, Rod Ansell survived by hunting and trapping wild animals, improvising shelter and using all the bushman's skills he knew.

COROMANDEL
Pat Barr

India in the 1830s is a hot, uncomfortable place, where the East India Company still rules. Amelia and her new husband find themselves caught up in the animosities which seethe between the old order and the new.

THE SMALL PARTY
Lillian Beckwith

A frightening journey to safety begins for Ruth and her small party as their island is caught up in the dangers of armed insurrection.

THE WILDERNESS WALK
Sheila Bishop

Stifling unpleasant memories of a misbegotten romance in Cleave with Lord Francis Aubrey, Lavinia goes on holiday there with her sister. The two women are thrust into a romantic intrigue involving none other than Lord Francis.

THE RELUCTANT GUEST
Rosalind Brett

Ann Calvert went to spend a month on a South African farm with Theo Borland and his sister. They both proved to be different from her first idea of them, and there was Storr Peterson — the most disturbing man she had ever met.

ONE ENCHANTED SUMMER
Anne Tedlock Brooks

A tale of mystery and romance and a girl who found both during one enchanted summer.

CLOUD OVER MALVERTON
Nancy Buckingham

Dulcie soon realises that something is seriously wrong at Malverton, and when violence strikes she is horrified to find herself under suspicion of murder.

AFTER THOUGHTS
Max Bygraves

The Cockney entertainer tells stories of his East End childhood, of his RAF days, and his post-war showbusiness successes and friendships with fellow comedians.

MOONLIGHT AND MARCH ROSES
D. Y. Cameron

Lynn's search to trace a missing girl takes her to Spain, where she meets Clive Hendon. While untangling the situation, she untangles her emotions and decides on her own future.

NURSE ALICE IN LOVE
Theresa Charles

Accepting the post of nurse to little Fernie Sherrod, Alice Everton could not guess at the romance, suspense and danger which lay ahead at the Sherrod's isolated estate.

POIROT INVESTIGATES
Agatha Christie

Two things bind these eleven stories together — the brilliance and uncanny skill of the diminutive Belgian detective, and the stupidity of his Watson-like partner, Captain Hastings.

LET LOOSE THE TIGERS
Josephine Cox

Queenie promised to find the long-lost son of the frail, elderly murderess, Hannah Jason. But her enquiries threatened to unlock the cage where crucial secrets had long been held captive.

THE TWILIGHT MAN
Frank Gruber

Jim Rand lives alone in the California desert awaiting death. Into his hermit existence comes a teenage girl who blows both his past and his brief future wide open.

DOG IN THE DARK
Gerald Hammond

Jim Cunningham breeds and trains gun dogs, and his antagonism towards the devotees of show spaniels earns him many enemies. So when one of them is found murdered, the police are on his doorstep within hours.

THE RED KNIGHT
Geoffrey Moxon

When he finds himself a pawn on the chessboard of international espionage with his family in constant danger, Guy Trent becomes embroiled in moves and countermoves which may mean life or death for Western scientists.

Birmingham City Council
Public Libraries Department

DLSI

HOUSEHOLD LIBRARY SERVICE – BORROWER'S RECORD SHEET

1 2 3 4 5 6 7 8 9 10 11 12 13 14 15 16 17 18 19 20 21 22 23 24 25 26 27 28 29 30 31
32 33 34 35 36 37 38 39 40 41 42 43 44 45 46 47 48 49 50 51 52 53 54 55 56 57 58 59 60 61 62
63 64 65 66 67 68 69 70 71 72 73 74 75 76 77 78 79 80 81 82 83 84 85 86 87 88 89 90 91 92 93
94 95 96 97 98 99 100

101 102 103 104 105 106 107 108 109 110 111 112 113 114 115 116 117 118 119 120 121 122 123
124 125 126 127 128 129 130 131 132 133 134 135 136 137 138 139 140 141 142 143 144 145 146
147 148 149 150 151 152 153 154 155 156 157 158 159 160 161 162 163 164 165 166 167 168 169
170 171 172 173 174 175 176 177 178 179 180 181 182 183 184 185 186 187 188 189 190 191 192
193 194 195 196 197 198 199 200

201 202 203 204 205 206 207 208 209 210 211 212 213 214 215 216 217 218 219 220 221 222 223
224 225 226 227 228 229 230 231 232 233 234 235 236 237 238 239 240 241 242 243 244 245 246
247 248 249 250 251 252 253 254 255 256 257 258 259 260 261 262 263 264 265 266 267 268 269
270 271 272 273 274 275 276 277 278 279 280 281 282 283 284 285 286 287 288 289 290 291 292
293 294 295 296 297 298 299 300

301 302 303 304 305 306 307 308 309 310 311 312 313 314 315 316 317 318 319 320 321 322 323
324 325 326 327 328 329 330 331 332 333 334 335 336 337 338 339 340 341 342 343 344 345 346
347 348 349 350 351 352 353 354 355 356 357 358 359 360 361 362 363 364 365 366 367 368 369
370 371 372 373 374 375 376 377 378 379 380 381 382 383 384 385 386 387 388 389 390 391 392
393 394 395 396 397 398 399 400

401 402 403 404 405 406 407 408 409 410 411 412 413 414 415 416 417 418 419 420 421 422 423
424 425 426 427 428 429 430 431 432 433 434 435 436 437 438 439 440 441 442 443 444 445 446
447 448 449 450 451 452 453 454 455 456 457 458 459 460 461 462 463 464 465 466 467 468 469
470 471 472 473 474 475 476 477 478 479 480 481 482 483 484 485 486 487 488 489 490 491 492
493 494 495 496 497 498 499 500

501 502 503 504 505 506 507 508 509 510 511 512 513 514 515 516 517 518 519 520 521 522 523
524 525 526 527 528 529 530 531 532 533 534 535 536 537 538 539 540 541 542 543 544 545 546
547 548 549 550 551 552 553 554 555 556 557 558 559 560 561 562 563 564 565 566 567 568 569
570 571 572 573 574 575 576 577 578 579 580 581 582 583 584 585 586 587 588 589 590 591 592
593 594 595 596 597 598 599 600

601 602 603 604 605 606 607 608 609 610 611 612 613 614 615 616 617 618 619 620 621 622 623
624 625 626 627 628 629 630 631 632 633 634 635 636 637 638 639 640 641 642 643 644 645 646
647 648 649 650 651 652 653 654 655 656 657 658 659 660 661 662 663 664 665 666 667 668 669
670 671 672 673 674 675 676 677 678 679 680 681 682 683 684 685 686 687 688 689 690 691 692
693 694 695 696 697 698 699 700

701 702 703 704 705 706 707 708 709 710 711 712 713 714 715 716 717 718 719 720 721 722 723
724 725 726 727 728 729 730 731 732 733 734 735 736 737 738 739 740 741 742 743 744 745 746
747 748 749 750 751 752 753 754 755 756 757 758 759 760 761 762 763 764 765 766 767 768 769
770 771 772 773 774 775 776 777 778 779 780 781 782 783 784 785 786 787 788 789 790 791 792
793 794 795 796 797 798 799 800

801 802 803 804 805 806 807 808 809 810 811 812 813 814 815 816 817 818 819 820 821 822 823
824 825 826 827 828 829 830 831 832 833 834 835 836 837 838 839 840 841 842 843 844 845 846
847 848 849 850 851 852 853 854 855 856 857 858 859 860 861 862 863 864 865 866 867 868 869
870 871 872 873 874 875 876 877 878 879 880 881 882 883 884 885 886 887 888 889 890 891 892
893 894 895 896 897 898 899 900

901 902 903 904 905 906 907 908 909 910 911 912 913 914 915 916 917 918 919 920 921 922 923
924 925 926 927 928 929 930 931 932 933 934 935 936 937 938 939 940 941 942 943 944 945 946
947 948 949 950 951 952 953 954 955 956 957 958 959 960 961 962 963 964 965 966 967 968 969
970 971 972 973 974 975 976 977 978 979 980 981 982 983 984 985 986 987 988 989 990 991 992
993 994 995 996 997 998 999 1000

1001 1002 1003 1004 1005 1006 1007 1008 1009 1010 1011 1012 1013 1014 1015 1016 1017 1018
1019 1020 1021 1022 1023 1024 1025 1026 1027 1028 1029 1030 1031 1032 1033 1034 1035 1036
1037 1038 1039 1040 1041 1042 1043 1044 1045 1046 1047 1048 1049 1050 1051 1052 1053 1054
1055 1056 1057 1058 1059 1060 1061 1062 1063 1064 1065 1066 1067 1068 1069 1070 1071 1072
1073 1074 1075 1076 1077 1078 1079 1080 1081 1082 1083 1084 1085 1086 1087 1088 1089 1090
1091 1092 1093 1094 1095 1096 1097 1098 1099 1100

1101 1102 1103 1104 1105 1106 1107 1108 1109 1110 1111 1112 1113 1114 1115 1116 1117 1118
1119 1120 1121 1122 1123 1124 1125 1126 1127 1128 1129 1130 1131 1132 1133 1134 1135 1136
1137 1138 1139 1140 1141 1142 1143 1144 1145 1146 1147 1148 1149 1150 1151 1152 1153 1154
1155 1156 1157 1158 1159 1160 1161 1162 1163 1164 1165 1166 1167 1168 1169 1170 1171 1172
1173 1174 1175 1176 1177 1178 1179 1180 1181 1182 1183 1184 1185 1186 1187 1188 1189 1190
1191 1192 1193 1194 1195 1196 1197 1198 1199 1200

1201 1202 1203 1204 1205 1206 1207 1208 1209 1210 1211 1212 1213 1214 1215 1216 1217 1218
1219 1220 1221 1222 1223 1224 1225 1226 1227 1228 1229 1230 1231 1232 1233 1234 1235 1236
1237 1238 1239 1240 1241 1242 1243 1244 1245 1246 1247 1248 1249 1250 1251 1252 1253 1254
1255 1256 1257 1258 1259 1260 1261 1262 1263 1264 1265 1266 1267 1268 1269 1270 1271 1272
1273 1274 1275 1276 1277 1278 1279 1280 1281 1282 1283 1284 1285 1286 1287 1288 1289 1290
1291 1292 1293 1294 1295 1296 1297 1298 1299 1300

1301 1302 1303 1304 1305 1306 1307 1308 1309 1310 1311 1312 1313 1314 1315 1316 1317 1318
1319 1320 1321 1322 1323 1324 1325 1326 1327 1328 1329 1330 1331 1332 1333 1334 1335 1336
1337 1338 1339 1340 1341 1342 1343 1344 1345 1346 1347 1348 1349 1350 1351 1352 1353 1354
1355 1356 1357 1358 1359 1360 1361 1362 1363 1364 1365 1366 1367 1368 1369 1370 1371 1372
1373 1374 1375 1376 1377 1378 1379 1380 1381 1382 1383 1384 1385 1386 1387 1388 1389 1390
1391 1392 1393 1394 1395 1396 1397 1398 1399 1400

1401 1402 1403 1404 1405 1406 1407 1408 1409 1410 1411 1412 1413 1414 1415 1416 1417 1418
1419 1420 1421 1422 1423 1424 1425 1426 1427 1428 1429 1430 1431 1432 1433 1434 1435 1436
1437 1438 1439 1440 1441 1442 1443 1444 1445 1446 1447 1448 1449 1450 1451 1452 1453 1454
1455 1456 1457 1458 1459 1460 1461 1462 1463 1464 1465 1466 1467 1468 1469 1470 1471 1472
1473 1474 1475 1476 1477 1478 1479 1480 1481 1482 1483 1484 1485 1486 1487 1488 1489 1490
1491 1492 1493 1494 1495 1496 1497 1498 1499 1500

1501 1502 1503 1504 1505 1506 1507 1508 1509 1510 1511 1512 1513 1514 1515 1516 1517 1518
1519 1520 1521 1522 1523 1524 1525 1526 1527 1528 1529 1530 1531 1532 1533 1534 1535 1536
1537 1538 1539 1540 1541 1542 1543 1544 1545 1546 1547 1548 1549 1550 1551 1552 1553 1554
1555 1556 1557 1558 1559 1560 1561 1562 1563 1564 1565 1566 1567 1568 1569 1570 1571 1572
1573 1574 1575 1576 1577 1578 1579 1580 1581 1582 1583 1584 1585 1586 1587 1588 1589 1590
1591 1592 1593 1594 1595 1596 1597 1598 1599 1600

1601 1602 1603 1604 1605 1606 1607 1608 1609 1610 1611 1612 1613 1614 1615 1616 1617 1618
1619 1620 1621 1622 1623 1624 1625 1626 1627 1628 1629 1630 1631 1632 1633 1634 1635 1636
1637 1638 1639 1640 1641 1642 1643 1644 1645 1646 1647 1648 1649 1650 1651 1652 1653 1654
1655 1656 1657 1658 1659 1660 1661 1662 1663 1664 1665 1666 1667 1668 1669 1670 1671 1672
1673 1674 1675 1676 1677 1678 1679 1680 1681 1682 1683 1684 1685 1686 1687 1688 1689 1690
1691 1692 1693 1694 1695 1696 1697 1698 1699 1700

1701 1702 1703 1704 1705 1706 1707 1708 1709 1710 1711 1712 1713 1714 1715 1716 1717 1718
1719 1720 1721 1722 1723 1724 1725 1726 1727 1728 1729 1730 1731 1732 1733 1734 1735 1736
1737 1738 1739 1740 1741 1742 1743 1744 1745 1746 1747 1748 1749 1750 1751 1752 1753 1754
1755 1756 1757 1758 1759 1760 1761 1762 1763 1764 1765 1766 1767 1768 1769 1770 1771 1772
1773 1774 1775 1776 1777 1778 1779 1780 1781 1782 1783 1784 1785 1786 1787 1788 1789 1790
1791 1792 1793 1794 1795 1796 1797 1798 1799 1800

1801 1802 1803 1804 1805 1806 1807 1808 1809 1810 1811 1812 1813 1814 1815 1816 1817 1818
1819 1820 1821 1822 1823 1824 1825 1826 1827 1828 1829 1830 1831 1832 1833 1834 1835 1836
1837 1838 1839 1840 1841 1842 1843 1844 1845 1846 1847 1848 1849 1850 1851 1852 1853 1854
1855 1856 1857 1858 1859 1860 1861 1862 1863 1864 1865 1866 1867 1868 1869 1870 1871 1872
1873 1874 1875 1876 1877 1878 1879 1880 1881 1882 1883 1884 1885 1886 1887 1888 1889 1891
1891 1892 1893 1894 1895 1896 1897 1898 1899 1900

1901 1902 1903 1904 1905 1906 1907 1908 1909 1910 1911 1912 1913 1914 1915 1916 1917 1918
1919 1920 1921 1922 1923 1924 1925 1926 1927 1928 1929 1930 1931 1932 1933 1934 1935 1936
1937 1938 1939 1940 1941 1942 1943 1944 1945 1946 1947 1948 1949 1950 1951 1952 1953 1954
1955 1956 1957 1958 1959 1960 1961 1962 1963 1964 1965 1966 1967 1968 1969 1970 1971 1972
1973 1974 1975 1976 1977 1978 1979 1980 1981 1982 1983 1984 1985 1986 1987 1988 1989 1990
1991 1992 1993 1994 1995 1996 1997 1998 1999 2000

2001 2002 2003 2004 2005 2006 2007 2008 2009 2010 2011 2012 2013 2014 2015 2016 2017 2018
2019 2020 2021 2022 2023 2024 2025 2026 2027 2028 2029 2030 2031 2032 2033 2034 2035 2036
2037 2038 2039 2040 2041 2042 2043 2044 2045 2046 2047 2048 2049 2050 2051 2052 2053 2054
2055 2056 2057 2058 2059 2060 2061 2062 2063 2064 2065 2066 2067 2068 2069 2070 2071 2072
2073 2074 2075 2076 2077 2078 2079 2080 2081 2082 2083 2084 2085 2086 2087 2088 2089 2090
2091 2092 2093 2094 2095 2096 2097 2098 2099 2100

2101 2102 2103 2104 2105 2106 2107 2108 2109 2110 2111 2112 2113 2114 2115 2116 2117 2118
2119 2120 2121 2122 2123 2124 2125 2126 2127 2128 2129 2130 2131 2132 2133 2134 2135 2136
2137 2138 2139 2140 2141 2142 2143 2144 2145 2146 2147 2148 2149 2150 2151 2152 2153 2154
2155 2156 2157 2158 2159 2160 2161 2162 2163 2164 2165 2166 2167 2168 2169 2170 2171 2172
2173 2174 2175 2176 2177 2178 2179 2180 2181 2182 2183 2184 2185 2186 2187 2188 2189 2190
2191 2192 2193 2194 2195 2196 2197 2198 2199 2200

2201 2202 2203 2204 2205 2206 2207 2208 2209 2210 2211 2212 2213 2214 2215 2216 2217 2218
2219 2220 2221 2222 2223 2224 2225 2226 2227 2228 2229 2230 2231 2232 2233 2234 2235 2236
2237 2238 2239 2240 2241 2242 2243 2244 2245 2246 2247 2248 2249 2250 2251 2252 2253 2254
2255 2256 2257 2258 2259 2260 2261 2262 2263 2264 2265 2266 2267 2268 2269 2270 2271 2272
2273 2274 2275 2276 2277 2278 2279 2280 2281 2282 2283 2284 2285 2286 2287 2288 2289 2290
2291 2292 2293 2294 2295 2296 2297 2298 2299 2300

2301 2302 2303 2304 2305 2306 2307 2308 2309 2310 2311 2312 2313 2314 2315 2316 2317 2318
2319 2320 2321 2322 2323 2324 2325 2326 2327 2328 2329 2330 2331 2332 2333 2334 2335 2336
2337 2338 2339 2340 2341 2342 2343 2344 2345 2346 2347 2348 2349 2350 2351 2352 2353 2354
2355 2356 2357 2358 2359 2360 2361 2362 2363 2364 2365 2366 2367 2368 2369 2370 2371 2372
2373 2374 2375 2376 2377 2378 2379 2380 2381 2382 2383 2384 2385 2386 2387 2388 2389 2390
2391 2392 2393 2394 2395 2396 2397 2398 2399 2400

2401 2402 2403 2404 2405 2406 2407 2408 2409 2410 2411 2412 2413 2414 2415 2416 2417 2418
2419 2420 2421 2422 2423 2424 2425 2426 2427 2428 2429 2430 2431 2432 2433 2434 2435 2436
2437 2438 2439 2440 2441 2442 2443 2444 2445 2446 2447 2448 2449 2450 2451 2452 2453 2454
2455 2456 2457 2458 2459 2460 2461 2462 2463 2464 2465 2466 2467 2468 2469 2470 2471 2472
2473 2474 2475 2476 2477 2478 2479 2480 2481 2482 2483 2484 2485 2486 2487 2488 2489 2490
2491 2492 2493 2494 2495 2496 2497 2498 2499 2500

2501 2502 2503 2504 2505 2506 2507 2508 2509 2510 2511 2512 2513 2514 2515 2516 2517 2518
2519 2520 2521 2522 2523 2524 2525 2526 2527 2528 2529 2530 2531 2532 2533 2534 2535 2536
2537 2538 2539 2540 2541 2542 2543 2544 2545 2546 2547 2548 2549 2550 2551 2552 2553 2554
2555 2556 2557 2558 2559 2560 2561 2562 2563 2564 2565 2566 2567 2568 2569 2570 2571 2572
2573 2574 2575 2576 2577 2578 2579 2580 2581 2582 2583 2584 2585 2586 2587 2588 2589 2590
2591 2592 2593 2594 2595 2596 2597 2598 2599 2600

2601 2602 2603 2604 2605 2606 2607 2608 2609 2610 2611 2612 2613 2614 2615 2616 2617 2618
2619 2620 2621 2622 2623 2624 2625 2626 2627 2628 2629 2630 2631 2632 2633 2634 2635 2636
2637 2638 2639 2640 2641 2642 2643 2644 2645 2646 2647 2648 2649 2650 2651 2652 2653 2654
2655 2656 2657 2658 2659 2660 2661 2662 2663 2664 2665 2666 2667 2668 2669 2670 2671 2672
2673 2674 2675 2676 2677 2678 2679 2680 2681 2682 2683 2684 2685 2686 2687 2688 2689 2690
2691 2692 2693 2694 2695 2696 2697 2698 2699 2700

2701 2702 2703 2704 2705 2706 2707 2708 2709 2710 2711 2712 2713 2714 2715 2716 2717 2718
2719 2720 2721 2722 2723 2724 2725 2726 2727 2728 2729 2730 2731 2732 2733 2734 2735 2736
2737 2738 2739 2740 2741 2742 2743 2744 2745 2746 2747 2748 2749 2750 2751 2752 2753 2754
2755 2756 2757 2758 2759 2760 2761 2762 2763 2764 2765 2766 2767 2768 2769 2770 2771 2772
2773 2774 2775 2776 2777 2778 2779 2780 2781 2782 2783 2784 2785 2786 2787 2788 2789 2790
2791 2792 2793 2794 2795 2796 2797 2798 2799 2800

2801 2802 2803 2804 2805 2806 2807 2808 2809 2810 2811 2812 2813 2814 2815 2816 2817 2818
2819 2820 2821 2822 2823 2824 2825 2826 2827 2828 2829 2830 2831 2832 2833 2834 2835 2836
2837 2838 2839 2840 2841 2842 2843 2844 2845 2846 2847 2848 2849 2850 2851 2852 2853 2854
2855 2856 2857 2858 2859 2860 2861 2862 2863 2864 2865 2866 2867 2868 2869 2870 2871 2872
2873 2874 2875 2876 2877 2878 2879 2880 2881 2882 2883 2884 2885 2886 2887 2888 2889 2890
2891 2892 2893 2894 2895 2896 2897 2898 2899 2900

2901 2902 2903 2904 2905 2906 2907 2908 2909 2910 2911 2912 2913 2914 2915 2916 2917 291
2919 2920 2921 2922 2923 2924 2925 2926 2927 2928 2929 2930 2931 2932 2933 2934 2935 29
2937 2938 2939 2940 2941 2942 2943 2944 2945 2946 2947 2948 2949 2950 2951 2952 2953 2
2955 2956 2957 2958 2959 2960 2961 2962 2963 2964 2965 2966 2967 2968 2969 2970 2971
2973 2974 2975 2976 2977 2978 2979 2980 2981 2982 2983 2984 2985 2986 2987 2988 2989
2991 2992 2993 2994 2995 2996 2997 2998 2999 3000